Piglettes

Clémentine Beauvais

PUSHKIN PRESS

Pushkin Press
71–75 Shelton Street
London, WC2H 9JQ

Piglettes was first published as *Les Petites Reines* by Éditions Sarbacane, Paris, 2014

First published by Pushkin Press in 2017

10 9 8 7 6 5 4 3 2 1

9781782691204

Designed and typeset by Tetragon, London
Printed and bound by CPI Group (UK), Croydon, CRO 4YY

www.pushkinpress.com

PIGLETTES

*To my favourite dwellers of
Bourg-en-Bresse, who fleetingly
appear throughout this novel*

PART I

Bourg-en-Bresse

I

Here we go: the Pig Pageant results have just come out on Facebook. I'm in third place: bronze medal.

How perplexing. After winning gold for two years in a row, I thought I'd never lose the top spot. I was wrong.

I check who's won the grand title. She's a new girl, in Year 11—I've never met her. Her name is Astrid Blomvall. She's blonde, pimply, and squints so much that you can only see half of her left pupil; the rest is tucked under her eyelid. The jury's choice is perfectly understandable.

A little Year 8 has won silver: Hakima Idriss. She is, indeed, very ugly too, with her black moustache and her triple chin; she looks like a pug.

Our dear friend Malo has left comments on each of the eighteen shortlisted girls' pictures. He paid special tribute to me:

Competition was fierce, but Mireille Laplanche, whatever the final results, will always be to me the most legendary Pig Pageant winner. Her fat blubbery bum, her droopy breasts, her potato-shaped chin and her tiny porcine eyes will remain imprinted in our memories for ever.

There were already lots of likes (78).

I added mine (79).

Then I tumbled downstairs into the living room and told Mum, "I won bronze this year!"

"Right. And what should I do, congratulate you?"

"I don't know. Would you rather I'd kept my gold medal?"

"I'd rather you'd never won the Pig Pageant at all."

"Then maybe you shouldn't have slept with an ugly old man."

"Don't speak ill of your father."

"Maybe he'd be proud of me!"

"He wouldn't be proud."

"I'm going to send him a letter."

"Don't send him a letter."

"'Dear Daddy darling, as yet another lovely school year draws to a close, your beloved daughter has won the bronze medal in the Pig Pageant organized annually at the Marie Darrieussecq High School in Bourg-en-Bresse. It is a happy disappointment, for she usually claims the top spot in that competition.'"

"Mireille, you're getting on my nerves." She rolls her eyes, and confides in the Habitat ceiling lamp: "I don't like teenagers."

My father is half French, half German. For confidentiality purposes, I shall call him here Klaus Von Strudel. A professor at the Sorbonne University in Paris, Klaus writes philosophy books. He was also my mother's supervisor for her doctoral thesis, and supervised her so well that she

12

ended up pregnant with me. Alas, their relationship was to remain forever secret! For Klaus was at the time—and still is—the husband of someone with a lot of potential. The proof: that someone has now been the president of our beautiful country of France for the past two years. I will call her, to keep things simple, Barack Obamette.

Barack Obamette and Klaus Von Strudel have three sons, who are therefore my half-brothers, and who have moronic Greek-hero names, but I shall refer to them here under the friendlier pseudonyms of Huey, Dewey and Louie.

For reasons beyond my understanding, Mum left Paris when she found out she was pregnant; she decided to become a philosophy teacher in Bourg-en-Bresse, which is the capital of the department of Ain (pronounced, not coincidentally, like that noise you make when you get a painful surprise). She has married a Monsieur Philippe Dumont, who is as bland as his name indicates. The three of us live together in a cosy detached house with a garden, in the pleasant company of the dog Kittycat and the cat Fluffles.

Am I in touch with Klaus? I am not, because he's never replied to any of my letters. Instead of replying to his secret daughter, he gives interviews to *Philosophy Magazine*. He also produces, roughly once every three years, a metaphysical treatise. Mum buys it and reads it, and I read it too. She says, *You won't understand, Mireille, it's complicated*, but I read it anyway and I understand sometimes.

13

Klaus writes things like:

Speculative realism has helped *lubricate the way* towards a post-Kantian metaphysics...

Quentin Meillassoux's thought grabs contemporary metaphysics and gives it an *orgasmic shake-up*...

I reject, however, the possibility of a philosophy *castrated of* Plato and Descartes...

Me: "Klaus is a dirty old man, isn't he?"

Mum: "Stop it. For one, he isn't called Klaus, and secondly, you don't understand anything—his thinking is revolutionary, but you can't understand that; you just don't."

"Mum, he's comparing Plato and Descartes to a pair of balls."

"Fifteen!" Mum sighs. "Fifteen! The stupidest age in the world."

"Fifteen and a half, if you please."

Aged eight, I sent my first letter to Klaus:

> *Hello Sir,*
> *My mother (Patricia Laplanche) told me that*
> *you we're my father. I woud like to meet you in*
> *Paris and also meet [Huey and Dewey*]. I am*

---

* Louie hadn't been born yet.

at Laurent Gerra Primary Schol. I have good
mark's and I learnt to read at four year old.
Goodbye,
Mireille Laplanche.

Aged twelve, I sent a second letter:

Dear Sir,
You never replied to the letter I sent you some
time ago. It would have been nice of you, but
whatever. I'm in Year 8 at Marie Darrieussecq
High School. I'm top of my class. I'd still like
to meet you, in Paris or elsewhere. My mobile
number is [...]
Sincerely,
Mireille.

I sent the third one a few months ago.

[Klaus],
You are my father. You know it, because you
must have received my first two letters. I see you
all the time on TV with [Barack Obamette] and
[Huey, Dewey and Louie]. To be honest I think
it's pretty shameful that you're not replying to
me. I'm fifteen, I'm not an idiot. In case you're
worried, my mother isn't "making me do this".
I've read all your books. Call me.
Mireille.

15

Still no reply. Mum knows perfectly well about that last letter, since I left the envelope casually resting on the kitchen table before posting it, with the following address:

[Klaus Von Strudel]
Presidential Palace of the Élysée
Paris
Hurry up, Mr Postman, Daddy's waiting!

"Hilarious," said Mum. "Hilarious; how funny you are, my child! I'm crying with laughter."

"Do you think we should let her post it?" asked Philippe Dumont, looking worried (= pursed lip + fiddling with his cufflinks).

"Let her do whatever she likes, she just wants attention," said Mum. "He won't reply, anyway, so it absolutely doesn't matter."

Philippe Dumont's intensely sad that he's never filled the gap Klaus Von Strudel left in my life. He takes me to the cinema, to the museum and bowling. He lets me eat chestnut spread directly from the pot. He says, "You must see me as your father, Mireille! I am your father!" I put my hands around my mouth and I go, "*Khoooo... khaaaa...* I am your faaaaather..." Then he gets annoyed: "This is my house, Mireille! That's my sofa! You live in my home, I'll have you know." That's only partly true, since Mum owns half the house, but she hasn't finished paying back the mortgage because of her teeny teacher's salary, whereas Philippe is a solicitor and a member of the Rotary club.

"What's the Rotary club, Mum?"

"It's a club with members like Philippe, people with various jobs; they meet up, they talk about things, they introduce their children to one another."

Philippe tries to introduce me to people. "Let me introduce you to Patricia's daughter, Mireille."

Rotary club members are ab-so-lute-ly de-lighted to shake hands with Quasimodo above taramasalata canapés at the Christmas party. One day, I must have been around nine years old, an extraordinarily shrewd person remarked, "This little girl looks strangely like that philosopher, you know, erm?"

I had a sudden flash of hope; I stared at that rosy-cheeked, flabby man and prayed, *Come on, say it, say I look like Klaus Von Strudel, sow the seeds of suspicion, let people think about the dates... Maybe if the whole of Bourg-en-Bresse petitions Klaus, he'll publicly recognize I'm his daughter!*

Instead of that, a lady suggested, "Jean-Paul Sartre?"

The man nodded vigorously, "That's it! Jean-Paul Sartre!"

"That's not exactly flattering!" the lady laughed.

"No," said the man candidly.

Google → Jean-Paul Sartre → squinty old man, atrociously ugly. Perhaps even uglier than Klaus.

I told Mum the next morning: "If you'd met Jean-Paul Sartre, I bet you'd have ended up in bed with him."

"Do you want a slap?"

17

"I'm just saying he's your type, that's all! A philosopher, revolutionary theory, blah blah... It's a compliment, Mummy! Why do you always take things the wrong way?"

"Don't be obnoxious. I don't spend my time sleeping around, with philosophers or anyone else."

"Well anyway, listen, he's dead," I said. "He died in 1980, Jean-Paul Sartre. And I was born hundreds of years later, so there's no doubt here—he's not my dad."

"Indeed he is not," Mum groaned.

I sang the Funeral March (taaah-taah-tadaahh-taaah-tadaaah-tadaah-tadaah) for a very long time to pay tribute to the memory of Jean-Paul Sartre. Mum started getting a bit twitchy about it: "Shut up, Mireille, you're giving everyone a headache," etc.

Then I said something I shouldn't have. "You know what we learnt in History, Mummy? After the Second World War, the French women who'd slept with Germans all had their hair shaved off as punishment. So imagine, just a few years earlier, you could have..."

She stared at me, looking like she was trying to process what I was saying, in utter disbelief. It unsettled me a bit, but I finished, as a joke:

"...lost your pretty curls!"

Slap.

"Go to your room. I don't want to see you here."

I don't know why I like to wind my mother up like that. I don't know why I poured the contents of that bottle of Flower by Kenzo perfume, which Philippe Dumont had so thoughtfully picked for my birthday

("Mireille, have you thanked Philippe for the perfume he so thoughtfully picked for your birthday?") down the toilet. And I made sure not to flush, so as to make it very clear that his fifty-four euros of fragrance had ended up down the drain.

I don't know why, but that's how it is.

*R*heumy: *adj. Full of rheum.*

A rheumy eye.

A rheumy eye is an eye full of that white and glutinous substance that eyes secrete. It's an eye that is kind of glued shut with its own ocular diarrhoea.

Such an eye is staring at me through the night-brown kitchen window.

"What the hell is that?"

That knocks on the window; I drop the kitchen roll, which unrolls all the way to the French window leading from the kitchen to the garden, like a red carpet (except it's white). I walk along it to open the French window.

The visitor is the Pig Pageant's gold-medal winner: Astrid Blomvall. Swaying from one foot to the other, in the dark garden, she fixes me with her eyes, her extremely rheumy eyes (especially the left one). She's wearing dark-blue jeans, much too tight, and a black T-shirt that says INDOCHINE at the top with a faded picture underneath showing a bunch of grumpy-looking men, and she's got two chunky arms sticking out of her T-shirt, arms that are pink and soft and pimply, and above all that, a fat pink face, framed with thick blonde hair like the string around a joint of meat, tied into a ponytail, and there's a dimple on her left cheek, a dimple that is the redemption of this flabby face, a dimple which, as Astrid Blomvall smiles, seems to invite all the tenderness of the world to come and nestle in it.

Just after smiling, as if hyper-aware of her braces, Astrid Blomvall looks down at her feet (which are securely strapped into a pair of hiking sandals).

"Hi," she mutters. "Sorry, hi, sorry, but I was wondering if maybe you were Mireille Laplanche by any chance, sorry for bothering you, I know it's late, I found your address on WhitePages.fr."

"Look, Astrid, let's make things very clear here," I say, letting her into my kitchen and onto the red carpet that is white. "You don't need to be sorry about anything. You stole my gold medal, sure! But I don't resent you. I think a bit of competition is a healthy thing in life. I think everyone should get their chance."

She stares at me fixedly (well, with one eye; the second one is hidden inside her eyelid). Hmm. Apparently, she doesn't get that I'm joking; people don't often get it when I'm joking. And now she's crying. Flood alert! Get the sandbags out, build the defences!

"Don't cry, Astrid Blomvall. Do you hear me, gentle damsel? Don't cry, or you'll get morbidly dehydrated. There, there, blow your nose."

I kneel down to tear a few squares off the white red carpet, and I offer them to her like you would an engagement ring. She blows her nose emphatically. I sit her down onto an Ikea stool that creaks rudely under her weight. The cat Fluffles, thinking I'm the one sitting down (since the stool is just as rude when *I* sit down on it), runs into the kitchen and jumps onto Astrid Blomvall's lap. Mindlessly, she starts stroking his back, which makes Fluffles lift his tail and show her his tiny little light-brown arsehole. Then he turns around to lick the tears running down Astrid's face. It's a kind gesture, but a slightly unpleasant one too, because his tongue is like a little strip of Velcro.

I introduce them to each other. "My cat Fluffles. Astrid Blomvall. Why are you crying, Astrid?"

"I've won the Pig Pageant," Astrid cries. "Is that not a good enough reason to cry? I've been in France barely a year; I've only been in Bourg-en-Bresse a little while, and I've already been voted top pig of my school!"

"Where were you before?"

"In Switzerland, with the sisters."

"What sisters?"

"Sisters, you know: nuns. In a Catholic school."

"Blimey!" I wince, shaking my hands to express how unconvinced I am by her parents' educational choices. What do her parents do, by the way? I enquire.

"My mum's an artisanal potter, my dad's a Swede."

"Does that offer good career prospects, being a Swede?"

"I mean he's Swedish and lives in Sweden and everything. He does things, I'm not sure what."

"I hope he's not the Swede who designed this Ikea

22

stool," I reply, pointing sternly at the object in question. "It's too small for even one of my bum cheeks, and loudly lets me know about it every bloody time I sit on it."

"You're funny," says Astrid thoughtfully.

Since I'm not just funny but also generous, I give her some Fanta. Then a bit of leftover cooked ham. Then a slice of home-made tiramisu—I tell her I made it myself with my little hands; she says I'm a good cook.

"It's because my grandparents have a restaurant. I fell into it when I was a child, like Obelix. Which might explain the comparable BMI."

"I'm not a good cook," says Astrid, "but I make good apple purée."

Then, "How do you deal with it, winning the Pig Pageant at Marie Darrieussecq? It's hard... It's really hard, seriously."

"Oh, I'm amazingly good at not taking things seriously. I know that my life will be much better when I'm twenty-five; in the meantime, I can wait. I have a lot of patience."

"It's sad to have to wait so long for things to get better."

I want to say, *Oh, only the first three years. Then you get used to it.* But clearly poor Astrid, at her Catholic school, hasn't had the same training as me; it's unlikely she got told often enough that she's *fatandugly*. Whereas it's happened to *me* so many times that I quite simply laugh it off. It runs off me like water from a lotus leaf.

Except sometimes when I'm a bit tired, or on my period, or if I have a cold; then, all right, sometimes I get slightly less watertight. But not tonight. Tonight I'm fine, and the Pig Pageant winner needs me.

Astrid fiddles with her T-shirt. The sad little men on the picture crumble away even more. Me: "You might not like what I'm going to say, but I think your T-shirt is on its last legs."

"It's because I wear it all the time."

Funny, that passionate voice, all of a sudden... and that now-legendary dimple, scooped out of her doughy face, as if by a teaspoon...

"Why?"

"Because Indochine are my whole life... My whole life. Tonight, I listened to them again before coming over here. They're the ones who gave me the strength to come and see you."

"Right. And supposing I don't know who Indochine are?"

She looks at me like I've just said I don't know who Barack Obamette is. I suggest: "Are they a boy band?"

"No! No, they're a rock group, they... You really don't know? They're... they're the best band in the whole history of the world!" She starts singing: "*And three nights every week, it's her skin against my skin*... No?"

"No, sorry. My mother doesn't listen to music and Philippe Dumont doesn't either, and I only listen to... well, not much, really."

I don't have a musical ear. My ears are too small, ugly and complicated to catch melodies—I think that, in order to enjoy music, you must need very long sideburns that

24

flap in the wind and funnel notes all the way down a vast, oyster-shaped ear.

"Who's Philippe Dumont?"

"A makeshift father and a synthetic husband; a handsome man with greying temples, well known to the local middle class, and fond of trips to Venice, from which he comes back with Murano vases that look like multicoloured glass vomit."

I point at one of them on the windowsill, which currently hosts a long arum lily sticking out its tongue.

"Cool," says Astrid, unconvinced. "But tell me, Mireille, what did you do, the first time you won the Pig Pageant? Did you close your Facebook account?"

"God no! Are you crazy? I just ordered a Hawaiian pizza, which I ate while reading Kafka's *Metamorphosis* because we had a test on it the next day."

That's a lie; I'm not the kind to leave book-reading to the night before a test. But I can't tell poor Astrid the truth, which is that, that night, three years ago, after discovering I'd been awarded the gold medal in the Pig Pageant, I ate a Hawaiian pizza topped with tears and snot, and spent three hours watching videos of cats riding Roombas on YouTube.

"Who's that guy, Malo whatsisface?"

"A complete dickhead who will be very successful in life."

"But why... why..."

"Why is he so nasty?"

"Yes, why does he *do* this?"

"Because he's very stupid. Probably a birth defect. We were born on the same day, you see, in the same hospital in Bourg-en-Bresse, so I think that the nurses were too busy marvelling that I was the ugliest baby they'd ever seen to notice that baby Malo in the next room needed a bit more oxygen or whatever gas you need in order not to become an absolute arse."

That's another lie. Malo and I used to be good friends. In nursery and in primary school, he was neither stupid nor nasty. We had fun together. We'd make bogeys out of playdough. We'd go to each other's house all the time. We took baths together, had water fights and slapped each other with wet flannels. Then we ended up in the same primary school, and we still kept going to each other's house after school and playing *Mario Kart*. In Year 6 we gradually grew apart. He found friends who told him, "Bloody hell, Malo, your friend Mireille is so ugly. She's a proper minger." Little by little he started thinking, "Bloody hell, that's true, I took baths with that ugly girl. I had water fights with that minger." In high school, it was all over. First day of Year 7, I walked up to him.

I said, "Hi, Malo!"

He was with a group of boys who all reeked of that Lynx shower gel, the one with the advert in which naked girls rub themselves erotically on bottles of said shower gel, even though everyone knows that it stings the genitals atrociously when you put soap directly on them.

He replied, "Yeah, what?"

Me: "Nothing, just hi! You all right? I didn't get my postcard this summer... You didn't go to Brittany?"

Him: "Why are you talking to me, you fat cow?"

Me: "Moo!"

And I galloped away, taking care to stick my tongue out at him.

That's another lie.

I didn't go "Moo!" I didn't gallop away with superb wit and detachment. I just stayed standing there with my eyes wide open until my eyeballs fell back inside my skull. I heard them rolling around like snooker balls, and three hours later, when the school nurse managed to fish them out with sugar tongs and slotted them back into place, I recovered my sight in a world where I'd become a fat cow.

The fat cow was wearing a too-tight T-shirt, too-tight jeans and too-tight shoes. She didn't fit into her clothes or this world.

Anyway: I don't tell Astrid all that, of course, because she's very busy crying, the poor dear, on the Ikea stool, which shrieks out that she's too heavy; and she's allowed to, after all; I shed a few dozen tears back then too, but now I don't care any more; it was a long time ago, I was young.

"Oh, no, Fluffles! Don't throw up on Astrid!"

I fling the cat off the half-Swede at the very last second, as his little ribcage contracts and twitches; hardly has he reached the floor when he vomits up a shapeless little mound of hair, undigested food and thin blades of grass, and, seeing this, runs away at top speed.

27

"Sorry," I say to Astrid, and wipe the lump of sick with the rest of the red carpet that is white. "Don't worry, I know he was just licking your face, but it's got nothing to do with you. He's like that: he stuffs himself with grass from the garden as if he never got the message from Mother Nature that he's supposed to be a carnivore."

"Who are you talking to, Mireille?"

Mum walks into the kitchen. Astrid raises her eyes towards her, then looks at me, then stares at Mum again, then at me. She's probably wondering, like everyone else, through which bizarre twist of genetics a gnome like me crawled out of a Cate Blanchett lookalike.

"G-good evening, Madame Laplanche," Astrid stutters.

"Mum, Astrid, Astrid, Mum. Astrid, Mum, is the Pig Pageant winner this year. She stole my top spot. She was brought up by the sisters and is a fan of Indochine. Do you know Indochine?"

"Of course," Mum sighs. "I'm so sorry, Astrid; it's such a horrible contest. I've tried to get it banned, but the school can't do anything, since it's all happening online. Terrible, I know. I hope you're not too upset."

"Thank you, Madame Laplanche," Astrid whispers. "It's awful, because I've been here less than a year. I hardly know anyone here. I thought people would be nice."

"There are nice people in this town," Mum says. "Like Mireille. Stay with Mireille, she's nice. And strong."

Me: "Don't listen to her, Astrid: it's a dirty pack of lies. She complains all day long that she should have faked a giant migraine the night I was conceived!"

"It was a morning," says Mum.

She leaves the kitchen and I watch her go, taking care to pretend I'm not at all touched by the impromptu compliment—a rare occurrence with my super-strict mother. But maybe that's precisely what makes me scream, "I've got an idea! Why don't we go find the other little piggy? I bet she's sad too. Plus, she's a minuscule Year 8 who's likely to lack maturity and critical distance."

"It's late," says Astrid.

"Yes, but if she's seen the results, I doubt she's asleep."

We Google her family name: Idriss. There's only one address for that name in Bourg-en-Bresse, in the Les Vennes neighbourhood, on the other side of town. We explain to my parents that it's of the utmost importance that we go there immediately even though it's late, for the well-being of our co-winner. They let us go.

Philippe Dumont: "Do you want me to drive you there?"

Me: "No, thanks, darling Daddy, best dad in the world, daddy par excellence and king of true and real paternity. We still smell of Fluffles's vomit, so your BMW might refuse to let us in."

And anyway, we'd rather walk through the night, walk through the Bourg-en-Bresse night, walk and get to know each other better, Astrid Blomvall and me.

3

Tonight is one of those nights when the moon is small, green and hard like a pistachio. Bourg-en-Bresse, under the brown night sky, isn't looking its best, and it's a pity.

Do you know Bourg-en-Bresse? It's pronounced *Bourkenbress*, in case you're wondering. Bourg—*Bourk*— for short.

It's a pretty town, Bourg-en-Bresse, a pretty little provincial town with everything you'd want from a provincial town. Two bookshops, a newsagent that sells hologram bookmarks (dolphins, kittens and ponies). Cafes, restaurants, artisans who make traditional enamel jewellery, small shops with windows full of gigantic bras, hair salons from which—*whoosh!*—big clouds of freshly cut hair get brushed out onto the pavement. Beautiful old houses with old wooden beams, and new developments bearing large billboards: FOR SALE. Few people buy—they go to Lyons or Paris, or leave the town centre to live in big detached bungalows. Other buildings are empty, and wooden planks have been nailed to the windows of closed shops. COMMERCIAL SPACE TO RENT. Small parks where very old people scrunch up the sandy pebbles as they walk; where children hang from metal bars in the soft play area; where high-school kids smoke and look at their phones.

I like Bourg-en-Bresse, my lovely town, my beautiful canteen. It's a town that feeds its people well. There are bakeries with sugar tarts as wide as bike wheels, lumpy with pink pralines. There's Le Français, the brasserie so gilded and full of mirrors that your eyes water as you eat your *filet Pierre*—a pillow of raw beef so soft you can cut into it with your fork like a huge strawberry. There's my grandparents' restaurant, the Georges & Georgette, two Michelin stars, opposite the recently whitened church of Brou. There they serve whole frogs gurgling in puddles of parsley butter, heavy cast-iron pots containing shrivelled, smoky snails, enormous clumpy quenelles whistling with steam, baked pâtés in glassy jelly...

And cheese boards! Mould-dappled Bresse Bleu, cinder-dashed Morbier, extra-old Mimolette, red as brick, and lumpy fromage frais, sprinkled with chives, lavishly wrapped in thick cream...

And hemispheres of wine in the glasses—and then, when it's time for coffee, box after box of chocolates and glazed chestnuts...

And brioche and pies, *fougasses* and baguettes; breads of all shapes and sizes, stuffed with green olives, peppers, figs, onions, nuts or dry sausage; breads that are hot and spongy, stick to your teeth, drink the butter and the yellow wax of the foie gras...

So, yes—it's only to be expected that I might be a little bit chubbier than the red-haired model in the window of Sandy Hair Salon; not a surprise that I tend to pass on the "ZeroCal Sandwich" option at the canteen—two Krisprolls and a slice of 100 per cent organic chicken, 2 per cent fat, 1.2 per cent carbs. And not a surprise, Malo, that you should be so skinny and so nasty, spending the day, as you do, chewing greyish gum, in this town made entirely of sugar and of cheese...

We're walking in the Bourg-en-Bresse night, Astrid Blomvall and I, and she's calming down slightly. She's already begun to realize, I think, that it's not such a big deal to win the gold medal at the Pig Pageant, at least not when you've got other passions in your life. And she does, and it's not only Indochine.

"I play video games."

"Oh really? Like what?"

"Mostly management and strategy games."

"What are they?"

"For example, *Airport Manager*. Do you know *Airport Manager*? No?" (She flushes; you can tell it's her thing.) "In *Airport Manager*, you're in charge of an airport. A big airport, like an international airport. So you have to deal with everything—*everything*—flights, disgruntled passengers, shops... Sometimes there are planes that crash on the landing strips... Sometimes there are people, right—they just give malaria to *everyone*. Sometimes there are terrorists."

"Sounds bloody stressful to me! Why do you play that?"

"Yeah, it's stressful but it's great. You have to watch your budget, earn a lot of money, but also spend it intelligently, and if for instance you lose a passenger's luggage, or if you've let the paparazzi in when there's a star coming in their private jet, that's it! You have to pay fines, it ruins your account balance."

"Sounds like a right headache."

"Not as much as *Kitchen Rush*. In *Kitchen Rush*, you're the owner of a big fast-food chain—or of an über-posh restaurant (you get to pick)—and you have to manage everything! There can be salmonella in the food if the kitchens aren't clean—that's such a nightmare, I can't even tell you. There are people who post nasty comments on consumer websites, even if you're amazing. And the work inspectors come and check that you don't underpay your employees. And if a waiter drops a dish on top of a customer's head..."

"Right, I think I get it. It's weird, as hobbies go, but I get it."

"And how about you? What do you do when you're not at school?"

"I..."

[Honest replies, in order of frequency:
  1) I cuddle Fluffles.
  2) I read philosophy books written by *mein Vater*, and other books written by other people.
  3) I cook with recipes I find on the Internet.

33

4) I look for recipes on the Internet.
5) I write things, like stories. That's so secret that you'd better forget I said it. Go on, forget.]

I reply to Astrid, "Oh, things."

See, I have a sense of privacy, unlike her. I don't go about telling all my secrets to strangers with rheumy eyes who could gossip about me to anyone.

(I did, once upon a time, confide in a girl called Aude, who liked me so much that all her profile pictures on Facebook were of her and me together. Since she was so nice, I did her homework for her and I let her crib from my tests in class. I also told her everything about how unhappy I was re Malo, for those were the days when I still cared, because I was young and immature. Unfortunately, my friendship with Aude went down the drain, firstly, when I realized that it was precisely *because* I was a pig that she loved pictures of her and me together—the contrast, it must be said, was staggering; next to me, she looked like a supermodel—and, secondly, when I found out that she was laughing about my Malodramatic life with her real friends while I was doing her homework at break.)

(Since then, I've learnt to be less trusting.)

We've reached Les Vennes. The short, square tower blocks are pierced by yellow rectangles, across which silhouettes occasionally pass.

"Isn't it a bit too late to knock on someone's door when we don't even know them?" Astrid asks.

She's right, it is 10.10. But in the Idrisses' building, almost all the lights are on. We check the intercom: they live on the third floor. We look up: a line of yellow windows, like a winning line at Connect 4.

Bzzzzzzzzz!

"Yes?" comes a warm, deep voice out of the star of dirty holes.

"Good evening. We're friends of Hakima's. Is she here?"

"*Friends* of Hakima's?"

The revelation seems to reduce Mr Warm and Deep Voice to incredulous silence for a few seconds. Then we hear: "Hakima! You've got friends here!"

(It is entirely possible that the exclamation mark is in fact a question mark.)

A small voice in the background: "*What?*"

"There are friends of yours here."

"*Who?*"

"Who?" asks the man with the enchanting voice.

I say mysteriously, "Two little piggies."

He repeats this to Hakima.

Silence.

Click, and the door opens.

"Third floor, left."

We pass by the lift and climb up the badly lit staircase, smelling of potato dauphinoise on the ground floor, pizza on the first, chicken curry on the second and chocolate cake on the third.

Grzzz! goes the doorbell when I press the little plastic disc, next to which a strip of paper reads IDRISS FAMILY.

The door opens. First it looks like there's nobody behind it. Then I look down, and I realize a god has opened the door.

4

Well, when I say a god, I don't mean an ugly old guy with a long white beard. I'm obviously not talking about the God of the Bible, who is zero per cent interesting. No, I mean the god of nature, the god of space, the god of bears, of cats and of cherries, the god who made the world by pinching the highest mountain tops into shape and by gouging out the vertiginous canyons with his mighty heels. The sun god who, every morning, drags a flaming star across the sky so that all life down below can grow!

No; not even the sun god: the Sun himself.

A blinding Sun.

And you know what—to see the Sun there, on the doorstep, it just—watch out, bad joke coming up—it just sweeps me off my feet!

Why is it a bad joke, Mireille? Because it so happens, dear reader, that the young man who's just opened the door has no legs.

Why not? I didn't find out straightaway. I was paralysed by shock and adoration.

So: the Sun bids us good evening gravely, and lets us

in, moving back his chariot, well, his wheelchair, by gently palming it on the side.

Astrid pushes me and I walk into the flat, breathing in deeply, since I've just fallen in love, after all, with the number one star in our solar system.

The flat, strewn with bright, warm fabrics, smells of a chocolate cake to die for. Hakima comes in, carrying said chocolate cake; clearly, she'd just taken it out of the oven when we rang the doorbell: it's still shrouded in steam.

Here she is, then, our third little piggy. She's littler than I thought, actually, and as shy as a sparrow. She gestures to us to sit around the coffee table to eat with them. I realize her eyes aren't red, unlike Astrid's. She has bags under them instead. Hasn't she been crying? Why is she so tired?

"Cake?" she offers.

"Oh, if it needs eating." I nod politely.

"I really shouldn't," sighs Astrid as if she'd just recently decided to go on a diet. "Ah well, all right then."

She couldn't have resisted long anyway: it's one of those cakes that are as runny as mature Camembert. Around the table, Hakima, her father and her mother are sitting on little pouffes, whose brown-leather cheeks are powdered yellow by the light of a nearby lamp. There's currently a solar eclipse, as Hakima's brother has vanished somewhere in the depths of the flat. The TV is muted, on LCI, a live news channel.

We introduce ourselves clumsily: Astrid Blomvall, Mireille Laplanche.

"You're not in Year 8," notes Madame Idriss.

38

"No," says Astrid.

"But you're friends with Hakima?"

"We are companions in despair," I explain. "It's all about that pig thing."

I realize I perhaps shouldn't have said that, because Hakima's parents are now enquiring about what pig-related thing her daughter could possibly have done. In Arabic, Hakima explains something which I translate in my head as: "No, Dad, I didn't have anything to do with pigs. It's those idiots at school who elected us pigs; it means ugly girls, it's an insult." They seem sad when she stops talking; Astrid lays a daring hand on Hakima's shoulder. But Hakima says to us: "I *do* care about that Pig Pageant, if you really need to know. But tonight, there are worse things on my mind. It's Kader's birthday. *[The Sun's name is Kader, the Sun's name is Kader!]* He's twenty-six. That's why I made a cake. But as we were about to light the candles, we saw the news, and now we don't want to light any candles any more; we don't want to celebrate anything any more."

"Why not? What did they say on the news?"

"Shush," interrupts Hakima. "Look."

She grabs the remote control, and the dramatic opening music of the evening news fills the room. Everyone watches.

Floods in Lorraine: a man saved an old lady who'd fallen into the water. There's an exclusive interview with the hero, while the camera focuses on a meowing kitten perched on a floating suitcase.

A baby was born with three arms in Montauban, but the doctors managed to cut one off so there would only be two left. The parents are expressing their gratitude.

And finally, the headline Hakima and her family were waiting for—the headline that ruined Kader's birthday...

"The programme of the Bastille Day garden party, given by the president of the Republic in the Élysée Palace on 14th July, has now been announced. On the list of famous people to be given the Legion of Honour medal that day are French Canadian singer Vanilla Jones, fashion designer Jacques Pacôme and the war hero general..."

For the purposes of this narrative, I suggest we call him General *Sassin*, first name Auguste, Auguste Sassin, A. Sassin, therefore, to his closest friends. This general is famous for his feats during the war in a sandy country we shall refer to here as Problemistan. Hearing the name of that general preceded by the phrase *war hero*, Hakima's parents quite simply begin to cry. Hakima, meanwhile, chews her slice of cake as if it were General Sassin's left cheek.

The famous people's pictures flash up in turn on the screen, followed by archive videos of the Élysée Palace, of Barack Obamette and, of course, of my own flesh-and-blood father, Klaus Von Strudel, alongside Huey, Louie and Dewey, waving to their people.

"The soundtrack for the Élysée garden party will be provided by the best of French pop-rock music, with an evening concert by—for the first time in *years*—Indochine!"

You don't say! Indochine! Upon hearing this, and as the next ten seconds are used to play a few notes from said band, our Astrid erupts into a joyful but inappropriate dance, which she contains as discreetly as she can, so as not to spoil the gloomy atmosphere.

A few minutes later—following the discreet mini-dance and the end of the crying fit—Hakima and her parents explain to us why the news has saddened and shocked them. It's because it's got something to do with why the Sun, aka Kader, no longer has any legs.

The Sun no longer has any legs because he lost them in a desert.

The Sun was in a desert because he was a soldier in Problemistan, where the president who preceded Barack Obamette had sent the army in order to bury desert people under sand dunes in order to prevent said desert people from exploding the Eiffel Tower with bombs hidden in fake pregnant women's bellies.

One day, the Sun, who'd recently been promoted to leader of a group of khaki soldiers, was on a mission. They'd just visited some people in square houses to make sure there weren't any weapons between their pots and pans, and the Sun now had to lead the troop through sabre-sharp mountains to reach a military base. The landscape was strewn with big brown rocks, like chunks of chocolate broken by a giant.

The sky was so white that day that it had exploded into a myriad little marbles of light. Under his helmet, the Sun squinted. Suddenly, he heard a little *ping*, sharp,

41

like a pebble on a car windscreen. He didn't worry about it straightaway. He only started to worry when his friend Laurent, who was standing next to him, fell face-first to the floor.

There was another *ping*, then another; then a much louder burst.

It seemed to the Sun that his vision had narrowed: everything had gone black, apart from a small bright disc of light framing some white, curious mountains. His legs went into autopilot.

As he let his legs run, the Sun wondered how the desert people could have known that they'd come this way today, when the general in charge of the mission, General Sassin, had promised him that the path would be clear, that the only dangers would be the heat and the chunks of rocks scattered across the valley.

General Sassin wasn't there; he was at the other military base, the one the troops had set out from the previous night.

The Sun was sad to have wasted his last minutes of life thinking about General Sassin as the shots ricocheted around him. In the end, one or two of them hit him, and he dropped to the sand like Laurent and all the others. He made sure he spent his last seconds of life thinking of his parents and his little sister.

But those turned out not to be his last seconds of life after all. He'd live to see his parents and his little sister again.

Not his legs, though.

———

Thinking back, I remember that story vaguely. The headlines: *Ten Soldiers Killed in an Ambush in Problemistan: One Miracle Survivor*. I hadn't given it much thought at the time: it was about politics and war; it mattered to me about as much as Philippe Dumont's first BMW. If I'd paid attention, I would have found out that the miracle survivor lived in Bourg-en-Bresse, in the Les Vennes neighbourhood; that he was now trapped in a wheelchair, and in his grief; that he had a warm, deep voice and a sister in a good position to win the Pig Pageant some day.

"And now," Hakima's mother groans, "that murderer Sassin is partying in the corridors of the Élysée... He's getting medals, even though he's responsible for the deaths of so many people. The internal inquiry isn't even over yet!"

"And meanwhile, Kader's been forgotten by everyone," adds Hakima's father. "It's the ultimate insult. The ultimate insult."

Hakima nods, and turns to us. "Yeah. You see, the Pig Pageant is bad. But *that*—that's what I care about."

Suddenly, a beam of light: the Sun reappears in the door frame. He joins us, at last, to nibble weakly on a piece of cake. I gaze at his large, severe forehead, his earthy eyes, his brown lips. I don't think I've ever seen someone looking so princely and so mineral. He ends up intercepting my glance, and asks sternly: "What's your name?"

"Mireille."

(A bright-beetroot Mireille.)

"Mireille, you're as pretty as a flower," says the Sun. "You're not a pig. Neither is my sister. And you're not, either," he adds to Astrid.

"Thank you, you neither," I stammer back. "You too, pretty as a flower. Not a pig at all."

He finishes his chocolate cake. I dare to stick my nose in. "But seriously, in spite of all that sadness... there's no reason not to celebrate your birthday."

"That's true," says the Sun's mother feebly. "Happy birthday, Kader."

"Happy birthday, Kader!"

We all kiss. We get up to kiss the Sun's cheeks. The Sun kisses my cheeks, accidentally setting them on fire. I sit down again with sirens ringing in my ears.

Hakima sighs: "I wish... I wish there was a way to go to that garden party, to tell the truth about Sassin, to scream it to all the journalists, to make them see it..."

"Hakima," growls the Sun.

At the same time, Astrid murmurs, "I wish... I wish I could see that Indochine gig..."

And I'm also whispering: "And *I*... I also have a reason, of sorts, to wish I could be there..."

Funny coincidence. Diverse, but... *related* reasons to be there, on 14th July, to interrupt their annual fiesta and—yes, why not—to remind *them* that we exist.

And while we're at it, we may as well do it with a bit of... *panache*, right?

———

That's how it happened. That's how the idea came to my mind.

It was Pig Pageant night, and I thought, why not?

Why not go up to Paris?

Why not get there on 14th July?

Why not gatecrash the president's garden party?

5

Often, at night, when I go down to the kitchen to get a cup of fennel tea in the vague hope that it might help me get to sleep, I hear Mum and Philippe Dumont talking, arguing or making up (oh, the horror). Tonight, thankfully, they're talking.

About me, as indeed they should be.

"That child isn't happy," Mum mutters. "I know it. She's suffering."

"That's normal, Patricia, she's a teenager."

"She writes—I know she writes. She writes things she doesn't show me."

"She's allowed to have little secrets. She's entitled to a life of her own, isn't she? You should let her be."

"She doesn't go out with friends. She doesn't have any friends. She locks herself in her bedroom; she doesn't want to go to the swimming pool—I can tell she's ashamed of her body. She doesn't want to wear nice clothes... It's almost as if she's trying her hardest to look ugly!"

"Patricia, she's fifteen and a half. At fifteen and a half, I was just like her—shy and awkward. And she's going through a kind of identity crisis, with that father who doesn't know she exists—it must have something to do with it."

"No, it doesn't," Mum snorts. "That's just something she's made up to make me feel guilty. She doesn't care about her father."

Enough is enough; in order to interrupt their little debate, I start talking, too—with the first creature I can find.

"Oh, Fluffles darling! You know, I'm so worried about Mum!"

I put on a high-pitched voice for Fluffles, not unlike that of the Siamese cats in *Lady and the Tramp*: "Wrrrhhhyy, Mirrrreille? Wrrrhhhy are you worrrrrried?"

"Because she writes! She writes stuff she won't show to anyone, not even to Philippe Dumont! I saw her hide a huge manuscript in her desk drawer the other day!"

"You should let her live her life, Meaaaorreille! She's entitled to a life of her owwwrrrn..."

The door opens; a rug of light unrolls into the corridor. My mother, in a pale-blue nightgown, pointy nipples under smoke-thin lace. "Very funny, Mireille."

"Oh, hi. I'm just chatting to my cat. Say hello to Grandma, Fluffles."

"Hellllrooo, Grrrrrandmaaaow!" (I lean down to help him wave his little paw.)

"I can't believe you rummaged through my desk drawers."

"Me, rummage? No need to be a world-class potholer to find your massive book next to the Sellotape. *Being and*

47

Bewilderment by Patricia Laplanche. *Towards a Philosophy of the Unexpected*. Great title! What's it about?"

"It's time to sleep, Mireille."

"Have you sent it to publishers?"

Oh, that sigh! A sigh that means *My daughter is so! My daughter is! Ah! She's so!* Sigh! "So far, if you really must know, I've sent it to just one publisher. Who rejected it."

"What!? They're complete morons! Which one was it? Gallimard?"

"What do you care?"

"If it's Gallimard, they're first-class losers. Seriously: a brick of Patricia Laplanche brain juice from concentrate, 300 pages, your face on the cover, and bingo—all the awards for Super-Intellectual Essay of the Year. I can already see the blurb on the front cover: 'the Catherine Zeta-Jones of philosophical thought'."

"Thank you, my darling, I will follow your extraordinarily insightful advice. I'm sure that, having been to Paris twice in your life, including once in my belly, you know everything about Parisian publishers, especially those specializing in essays on phenomenology."

"*PhenomenAlogy*, beloved Mummy; for you are *phenomenal*!" (Deep voice:) "During the week, she gives classes to spotty teenagers. At weekends, she writes phenomenalogy essays. This summer, on your screens: Patricia Laplanche, in *Phenomenal*."

"Sure. Well, *they* seem to think that as a high-school teacher in a provincial town, as opposed to a university lecturer in Paris, I'm not at all phenomenal."

"They're profoundly intellectually disturbed. Are you going to send it to other publishers?"

"It doesn't matter, Mireille."

Fluffles intervenes, waving his little paw: "Please, tell meeeaow, Grandmmmmma! Tell meeeaow!"

"Mireille, go to bed, it's late."

"Wait wait wait, I need to tell you something, Mummy. Listen to this crazy thing: it's amazing—tonight I've fallen in love with the Sun, and on top of that I've got two new friends. Not only that but also we're going to gatecrash the garden party at the Élysée Palace on 14th July—it's all sorted, we're just finalizing details to make sure it all goes smoothly because of the fact that General Sassin will be there, the one whose fault it is that the Sun's got no legs left; he's the brother of my new friend, by the way, well, one of the two, and anyway Indochine, the band that my other new friend loves, they'll be there too, so I need to listen to their songs, and also Klaus *mein Vater* will be there, and I'll be like, hey, you're my father and you'd better make amends for the condom accident! So, so, what do you think, Mum, what would you recommend, what would you say to me and the other two little piggies, how do you think we should go up to Paris and gatecrash the Élysée garden party, hey? What do you reckon?"

"You should cycle there, it'll give your calf muscles a workout."

Slam goes the door.

———

Philippe: What did she say? I didn't catch any of that. She got sunburn?

[Ah! If only you knew, Philippe Dumont! Is there a special after-sun cream for the heart out there that could save me?]

Mum: *Sigh.* Who knows what goes on in that child's head?

Philippe: But is it true, my darling? You wrote a philosophy book?

Mum: Oh, Philippe, please.

Philippe: No, but wait, it's great, all these years you've been saying—

Mum: I don't want to talk about it, and anyway, it doesn't matter. I'm tired.

Philippe: But have you sent it to—

Mum: Philippe! Let me sleep.

Click goes the light.

Smooch goes a not very passionate kiss signalling the improbability of a night of passion.

Splosh splash goes Kittycat the dog as he jumps onto the duvet cover, making said night of passion utterly impossible now. (Phew.)

On my side of the wall, a text is sent to Hakima and Astrid:

Beloved piggies—or, should I say, beloved piglettes; my mum has just given me the idea of the century. We're going to cycle there. Meet at 1.14 p.m. in my garage this Saturday.

6

There are three bikes in our garage, all of them mine. One was given to me by Philippe Dumont, another by my grandparents, the third by my mother. All three of them are nicely gathering dust, seemingly hanging from the ceiling by countless graceful cobwebs.

One is called Giant and is red and gold—the colours of Gryffindor. Its saddle is as high as its brakes, so you have to ride it with your bum sticking up in the air and your legs shaved, wearing an aerodynamic helmet (*all* things I love). Philippe Dumont gave it to me to compensate for the number one void in his existence: a son he could teach how to light a barbecue and call "buddy" while play-fighting.

The bike Grandpa Georges and Grandma Georgette gave me has no name; it's beige and uptight, with a curvy frame like an ivory pipe. It's a real show-off. There's a basket in the front and a slightly camp bell that goes *Drrring! Drrring!* The third bike was given to me by Mum. It's called Bicycool. Simple, royal-blue, comfortable; a bell that just goes *ting-ting!* and a luggage carrier on which one should never under any circumstances put any luggage, or else it will hang down and rub against the wheel, and then you're in a pickle.

And here they are, standing sadly surrounded by shovels, skis, broken bits of furniture, wellies, rat poison and firelighters—three skeletons, waiting for a brave hand to pull them out of their messy home, at which point they will immediately start shrieking that no, no, no, they don't want to go.

"They're a bit rusty," I note, lifting the wheel of the beige bike. "Don't get too close, Hakima, you'll catch tetanus."

Hakima takes a step back into the shadows, horrified. Astrid says, "What about me? Don't you care if *I* catch tetanus?"

"You've lived three years longer than Hakima—it'd be much less unfair. Here, help me get the red Giant, there. You have to lift the stand... *[clunk]* OK, no more stand. Wait, try to get the back wheel of the blue one... *[clang]* Ah well, we weren't going to use that luggage carrier anyway. Can you hold the red one for a minute? *[Pssssshhhhh]* Oh, yes, we'll have to inflate the tyres. And mend the punctures. And... apparently, change the wheel on that one, seeing as it's bent."

"Are you seriously pretending you can change a bike wheel?"

"Astrid, Astrid, stop seeing life in gloomy black and white. Always questions implying that we can't do this or that! I know very well how to change a wheel. You put it in a bucket of water, and when you see some bubbles coming up it's ready."

"That's how you make pasta."

"No, no, I'm telling you, there's a thing about bubbles."

"Yes, when you're fixing punctures on tyres, not when you're changing a wheel. OK, well—good thing I was a scout, and *I* can do it."

I sway with shock. "You were a scout, Astrid?"

"Of course. In the Swiss mountains, with the sisters. We'd go cycling all the time. And hiking in the hills. There were precipices everywhere. Once, we saw a sheep tumble down one of them. When it landed at the bottom it sounded like a pencil case falling off a desk."

Hakima goes "Ah!" with terror. I nod appreciatively. "And there was me thinking you only knew how to play *Chicken Run* and listen to Indochine."

"It's *Kitchen Rush*, not *Chicken Run*. Get me your dad's toolbox."

"It's not my dad's, it's Philippe Dumont's."

Philippe Dumont's toolbox is exactly like Philippe Dumont's DIY ambitions: big, but never put into action. He's only opened it once, to weigh up the different tools. Thus all of them are still tidily slotted into their respective holes, like a biscuit selection: an electric drill that looks like a small hairdryer; a smart screwdriver with detachable ends; a macho hammer, with a big handle; a cute hammer, with a small handle; a neon-orange crowbar; and lots of little magic drawers stuffed with nails, screws and hooks.

That reminds Hakima of something: "The other day, in Biology, we learnt that if you extracted all the iron from someone's body and put it all together, you could make a little nail out of it."

"Wow," I whistle. "I can't decide if that's too much or not enough."

"It's just right," Hakima states. "Just one little nail, no more."

Astrid intervenes. "Popeye must have more. At least one big nail, if not two."

"No, because we learnt that Popeye, actually, you know, that thing about the spinach, it's not true. There's not very much iron in spinach, but there's lots in broccoli and lentils."

"Oh, really? So what's Popeye's iron content like, then? A pin? A needle?"

Me: "Piglettes, focus, please. We need to change that wheel. Astrid, show us."

She shows us, and we watch her. She unscrews the wheel, slides it aside, straightens it up by hammering it something serious and puts it back into place. It looks like it's worked. She fetches a bucket of water...

(Me: "Ha! I knew there was a thing about a bucket of water!")

...dips the punctured tyre into it; bubbles appear...

(Me: "Bubbles! It's ready!")

...then she pulls the tyre out again, expertly patches up the punctures and pumps it up with surprising strength. Hakima and I watch her, bemused but happy, since

Astrid's doing all the work, huffing and sweating in the heat of the garage.

Then she oils the bike chains. Her white hands get coated in black grease, the gears click, the links jump into place. Watching those machines come to life is a beautiful thing; like creatures from a fairy tale, stretching and yawning after sixteen years of snoring, trapped by the terrible curse of Mireille's Legendary Laziness...

After a while, Astrid finally realizes that we're shamelessly freeloading, watching her do all the work without lifting a finger ourselves, so she gives us some chores to do. You screw this, you unscrew that, you oil this, you inflate that. Her orders are clear, precise and segmented into perfectly manageable slices. You can tell she's got a flair for management, thanks to all those extremely weird video games.

It's almost 3.47 p.m., and the bikes are fixed. We wheel them out into the garden.

"We're going to have to try them, now," says Astrid.

A wave of surprise washes over us, all of a sudden. We were sort of joking, the other day: the bike idea, the garden-party plan, the insanely long journey! We were acting as if we really meant it, but...

But now... the bikes are here, shining in the golden sunlight; they're whispering, *Why not?* They're waiting for us to ride them, to take them to Paris. They're already shuddering with impatience and excitement. The red-and-gold Giant wants to fly along open roads all the way to the capital, and up the Champs-Élysées like its mates in the Tour de France. The beige bike simpers, with its perfect curves and its *drrring drrring*; it wants us to take it on a tour of the Latin Quarter. And the little blue one is hoping for a quiet trip alongside rivers, on sandy paths, with evenings spent cooling down, after a warm day, locked to a tree near the three little piglettes' tent.

"Well... I guess we could *try*," says Hakima.

"If we don't like it, we can always give up," I add.

"We can just go on a tiny little ride," confirms Astrid.

As if it's the most natural choice for her, Hakima opts for the Giant. She perches up on the seat like a pigeon, her legs too short to touch the ground. The precarious balance doesn't seem to bother her. Astrid Blomvall, not a little proud of her work, bagsies the pretentious beige bike. That's perfect—the one that's left for me is Mum's, the small blue one, exactly the right size—Goldilocks's bike, if Goldilocks was a fat little piglette with straight chestnut hair.

And they're off! We're going for a spin.

Mum's in the garden, reading a big book in a deckchair, thighs caramelizing, bug-eye sunglasses on the end of her nose. Philippe Dumont has just finished mowing the lawn, which is so green and so clean that it looks like he's hoovered it. Both watch us pass by, marvelling at the miraculous sight.

"Mireille's *fixed* the bikes?"

"Mireille's *cycling*?"

Why, it seems pigs might actually fly after all. Mum stands up to watch us go—her tulip skirt, straw-yellow, billows in the breeze. Philippe comes to hold her by the waist. I spy on them discreetly as we ride down the alley; they're American-beautiful, with their sugar-coloured house, in their garden planted with bushes like Brussels sprouts.

Kittycat the dog, excited by the noise, runs over to us wagging his tail—but fails miserably at licking our calves. He quickly understands that we're champion cyclists and he won't be able to catch us (plus he's asthmatic). We're already far away, whooshing towards Bourg-en-Bresse town centre, we the piglettes, we the gatecrashers, on our pretty bikes that shriek with light and laughter.

I don't know if you've ridden a bike recently?

Maybe you do it all the time. In which case you might be too used to it to notice.

To notice the *magic*.

What's magical about a bike is that it's a broomstick—a flying broomstick that punches holes through the air, obeying your merest thoughts; it responds to your fingers, your feet, your groin; you don't need to tell a bike where to go, it knows—it's a flying broomstick.

What's magical about a bike is that it's also a horse. A proud, athletic horse—that hurts its hooves sometimes, that whinnies and grinds its teeth when it stumbles into a pothole; you have to stroke a bike and talk to it. You really must—it's a horse.

What's magical about a bike is that it's a clickety, metallic machine, a mechanical wonder; look at its gears and marvel.

And when you realize how magical a bike is, all those things begin to mingle within you, and all at once you can feel the air bursting as you tear through it, feel every crack and crease in the road, the most intimate hiccups of the bike's workings; and the blood inside you pumps harder with each pedal stroke.

And suddenly it all fuses together, and it's a miracle: everything is fast and fuzzy, and you are completely at one with the universe, as if you'd created it yourself.

7

Market day in Bourg-en-Bresse. Sweaty (Astrid and me pepper-coloured, Hakima the deep red-brown shade of a beef tomato), we leave our proud bikes locked together and to a lamp post.

I tell the piglettes, "Last time I went anywhere this fast was probably fifteen years ago, during a certain morning cuddle, when I left Klaus von Strudel to invade my mum's belly."

"But actually, that's not how it works," said Hakima, "because we learnt in Biology that, in fact, the sperm isn't, like, a tiny human or anything, it's just half, and it's only when it gets to the egg that it becomes cells, so actually it's not true when we think that the baby won the race against the other sperm."

"Glad you clarified that for us. Shall we have a wander round the market?"

The problem with that idea is that after a few steps, we start aching all over, and a few yards later, we're holding on to each other like a gang of winos outside a bar. At the same time, it's pretty funny—we sway through the crowd moaning *ouch ouch ouch* every time we lean on a muscle butchered by our twenty minutes of cycling, which causes quite a stir among the people weighing melons and tasting bits of goats' cheese.

"Crikey, Mireille, what's up with you?" asks Raymond, the cheese and charcuterie seller, from whom I buy garlands of sweaty *saucissons* and deliciously chalky Crottin de Chavignol every weekend.

N.B. There's only one thing you really need to know about me, which is that Crottin de Chavignol is my favourite cheese.

"We're aching all over, Raymond. We went cycling for at least eighteen and a half minutes!"

"Why would you do that to yourselves? Come on, let me help you get your strength back."

Today he's got a Papillon Roquefort like you'd never believe, a mortadella sausage so green and pink it looks Photoshopped, and tiny goats' cheeses like whitewashed buttons. He hands us out three of them with his big brown fingers; we gobble them up and thank him. Hakima politely says no to the next gift— small slices of roasted *figatelli* sausage—but she accepts the third: a cup of Normandy apple juice, painfully cold.

As we feverishly rub our throats to thaw them out, a customer comes in, and Raymond produces an enormous dish of...

"Pork sausages! Made from the juiciest, plumpest piggies in the region. Plain or thyme? Need apple sauce to put on the side? Ask Flavie over there, she's got the sweetest cooking apples you'll ever taste—you'll get diabetes just looking at them!"

Another voice, behind us: "*Juicy plump pigs?* I'd watch out if I were you..."

We turn around, throats still cryogenically frozen.

"The three juiciest, plumpest piggies in the region, together! How cute! Selfie!"

It's Malo. He leans towards us and takes a picture—his radiant face in the foreground, ours right behind him, in full chewing glory: cheeks full of cheese, foreheads drenched in sweat, red-dappled necks. No doubt the selfie will soon end up on Facebook, Twitter or Tumblr. #pigpageant.

Astrid and Hakima are frozen like a couple of rabbits in the headlights, clearly waiting for me to say something.

I say something. "Dear piglettes, let me introduce you to this blond paparazzo. His name is Malo. It is thanks to him that, every year, Marie Darrieussecq votes for its three juiciest, plumpest little piggies. The genius idea for this very original contest came to him three years ago, in the middle of a boring music lesson, while he was puffing into a recorder. He started by setting up a Facebook group, and then it all went very fast. Please note that this was no money-making venture—it's a labour of love of the purest kind."

Our contest organizer spits out a skinny thread of saliva, which lands on the floor next to a small Yorkshire terrier.

"Great to bump into you here. Birds of a feather, hey? Smelt the lard, felt at home?"

Please, I think very hard, *please, girls, please, don't start moaning that it's really not nice to say things like that; I beg you, please, don't start whining that you don't understand how anyone can say that sort of thing.*

"It's really not nice to say things like that," moans Astrid.

"I don't understand how anyone can say that sort of thing," whines Hakima.

Perfect. Malo revels in those magnificent moans and repeats them right back at us, in a mock-idiotic voice. The piglettes' eyes well with tears instantly. Mine don't—I have better windscreen wipers.

I try another tack. "When I think, Malo darling, that we got married for real in Reception, and we told each other we'd pretend we were really in love for ever and ever. Whatever happened to our vows?"

He laughs. "Never made any vow to any sow."

And he swings to the side to grab the waist (as waspish as they get) of a charming young lady who seems to be wearing a thick belt in lieu of a skirt and a bra in lieu of a top. But then she's got the body to make that kind of thing work, with a top like this: V, and legs like this: | |

"Look, Princess," says Malo. "It's the three pigs that won the pageant."

"No way!" yells Princess, eyes glued to her phone. "No way! Wait for it—wait for it—wait for it—so Pablo's just, like, calling me now, like, out of nowhere? Like, I'm like, what? What a dickhead! I mean, seriously?"

And *tick tick tick*, she power-texts Pablo on her iPhone, the case encrusted with splendid sticky crystals that burn the retinas of everyone in her immediate vicinity with their glitter. Her long, curvy nails click against the screen.

Hakima and Astrid are petrified. Astrid has probably never seen someone like Princess at the sisters', and Hakima's surprise seems to indicate that such a creature has never been invited home by the Sun either (phew!).

Malo, a little saddened to see Princess writing a novel to that dickhead Pablo, tries to take back control of the situation. "If Raymond manages to sell plump juicy pig sausages, maybe he can give you some tips on how to present yourselves better. Then maybe someone would take one of you off the shelf."

"What a *bitch*!" howls Princess behind him, still staring at her screen.

"Well, I suppose we *could* always try dipping ourselves in apple sauce," I reply. "With a bit of parsley on the side, and mashed potatoes..."

"Yeah, right, fill a bath with mashed potatoes and stick a sprig of parsley up your arse, it should get you some likes on YouPorn—after all, it's full of videos of naked dwarves and hairy women, it must turn on some peo—"

"NO WAY!" Princess explodes. And then starts crying with laughter. "Babes! Babes! Watch this!"

Malo "Babes" Delattre watches this, looking like someone who finds something not very funny but tries to pretend it's very funny with a classic this-is-not-very-funny-but-I'm-trying-super-hard-to-pretend-I-think-it's-hilarious expression.

"Did you *see* that? What a *bitch*!" howls Princess.

"What a bitch," Babes confirms.

Ping! Princess checks her email, and suddenly switches tab, and changes mood. "Forget it, let's go, Pablo's being a total loser."

I take advantage of the sombre atmosphere to chip in, "Lovely to meet you, Princess."

Princess lifts her nose for the first time, and fixes me with her dark-blue eyes, staring out of Cleopatra make-up.

Then: "Wow! What? Wow! I mean, just, like, *wow*!"

Upon which she sets off, pocketing her phone, and Malo follows her, yapping "Did you see how fugly they are, did you see?" but Princess is only moderately interested, probably because it's not as lame as whatever thing that bitch just posted.

"Before I forget—catch!" Malo shouts, and throws something to us. Hakima catches it like a rising star of the NBA.

As the duo disappear into the distance, I give the girls a telling-off.

"Right, darling piglettes, we're going to have to give your repartee muscles a serious workout. We're going to gatecrash the Élysée garden party, remember? The point is to do it scandalously and sensationally. It's not going to work if you have tongue paralysis."

I go back to Raymond to buy some ham and Rocamadour cheese. Astrid taps my shoulder. Tap, tap. Yes, just a second, Astrid. Tap, tap. I said just wait a sec, I'm paying. Well, hurry up. Yeah, calm down, I'm getting there! Here you go—what's the rush?

The thing Malo threw Hakima turns out to be a regional newspaper: the *Bresse Courier*. I know the editor-in-chief, who's a Rotary friend of Philippe Dumont's, but I've never met Hélène Lesnout, the author of today's headline article.

PARENTS PERPLEXED BY PIG PAGEANT

Ingrid, Fatima, Marielle.* Three ordinary teenagers, in Years 8 and 11 at Marie Darrieussecq High School in Bourg-en-Bresse. Three teenagers whose names are now on everyone's lips, ever since they were listed, last Wednesday, on a Facebook page—which awarded them gold, silver and bronze medals in the annual Pig Pageant, or in other words the school ugliness contest.

[full article on p. 3]

Flip, flop, flip, we turn to page 3.

At Marie Darrieussecq, the "pageant" is already in its third year—and none of the teenagers we meet outside the school seems particularly keen to stop it. "Sure, it's not very nice for the girls," says Nathan,* 13 years old, "but it won't kill them. It's just a joke." Alessia* and Oriane* disagree. "It's

65

really stressful. We try really hard to make sure we don't get shortlisted. It would be horrible."

Ms Cerdon, the school's head teacher, disapproves of the contest, but also stresses her powerlessness. "We can't do anything. It's on the Internet, it's not the school's responsibility. We've already tried talking to the student who started it all, but the most we can do is reiterate basic citizenship rules."

Who is the student who launched the Pig Pageant at Marie Darrieussecq three years ago? Marco,* a handsome, confident young man of 15, assures us that the contest is "a privilege" for the shortlisted girls. "It lets them know they should take more care of themselves." He also claims that the "finalists" of the past two years have "considerably improved" since their nominations. "Apart from one of them, who got yet another medal this year, the past laureates have lost a lot of weight and really looked after themselves. I think the contest showed them that they'd let themselves go."

Marco introduces us to Charlotte,* who was "awarded" a silver medal two years ago. Now in Year 11, the bubbly brunette confirms that the contest "was a real wake-up call. I finally saw what I'd refused to see until then: I was disgusting. Immediately afterwards I started exercising, I lost weight, I started following fashion blogs, I changed my hairstyle. I'm not saying the contest's a good thing, but without it, maybe I'd still be a pig."

* Names have been changed.

"Who's Charlotte?" asks Astrid, scratching her chin.

"Probably Chloé Ragondin," I reply. "She *has* changed a lot since she got that silver medal. She stopped eating cake, then she stopped eating meat, then she stopped eating altogether. Saves her money, I guess."

"Why didn't that journalist interview *us*?" whispers Hakima. "We're the ones at the centre of it all."

"You'd have agreed to be interviewed?" asks Astrid, a bit surprised. "I wouldn't. I'd never have known what to say."

"Me neither," says Hakima, "but we'd have sent Mireille, because Mireille always knows what to say."

"Yeah, tell me about it!" I growl. "You both mysteriously lost the gift of speech when Malo and Princess appeared! I felt like I was surrounded by piggy versions of the Little Mermaid!"

"You know we're not like you, Mireille," says Hakima limply. "We're not extrinsic."

"Extroverts."

"Yes, that. We've got *l'esprit de l'escalier*—staircase wit."

"What's that?" asks Astrid.

"We learnt it at school. It's, like, when you think of a witty reply to something someone's said, but the person you want to say it to, well, they're already gone."

"What's it got to do with staircases?" Astrid wants to know.

"Can't remember. Maybe something like, you're so gutted that you thought of the witty reply too late that you throw yourself down the stairs."

Astrid looks puzzled.

"To kill yourself," Hakima specifies.

Astrid coughs. I throw my plump juicy arms around my plump juicy friends. "Right, let's set things straight. No one's throwing themselves down any stairs in the name of any wit. We've got bikes, we've got calves, we've got a garden party to crash. We've got a villainous Malo to fight, who's in love with a Princess who cares more about her magic mirror than him. The stage is set for a true fairy-tale ending. And now, we've got something else too: media coverage. And we're going to use it."

"We've got what?" Hakima asks.

"Media coverage. Hakima, pay attention. You're the one who suggested the idea, I'll have you know."

"What idea?"

"You said we should be front-page news! Trending topics. Red-hot hashtags."

"Did I?"

I drag them out of the market, smiling at the Bourg-en-Bresse shoppers cramming their baskets full of vegetables, fruit, fish, cheeses and jars.

"We're going to get hold of that Hélène Lesnout, and she's going to write an article about us. I mean *really* about us, this time."

8

"Philidarling Daddy, Daddy Dumont extraordinaire, may I have a word?"

Philippe Dumont shoots me a strangely suspicious stare over the bowl full of lasagne filling he is energetically mixing. Mum, acting as if she hasn't heard, focuses on her pasta-making machine.

"What are you after?"

"I was just wondering if you happen to know a lady called Hélène Lesnout, seeing as you walk through life stuffing your pockets with new friends?"

Waiting for a reply, I stick my spoon into a tin of chestnut spread. The brown paste curves sensuously around it, leaving Philippe Dumont and Mum plenty of time to swap worried glances. On the sofa, Hakima and Astrid pretend to be playing with Fluffles, who isn't pretending to bite them.

"You saw the article," says Philippe Dumont.

"Yup! And we'd love to meet the journalist."

"Erm... what for?"

"To bash her head in with a snow shovel and dump her lifeless body in a ditch. No, just kidding. We'd like her to give us some free publicity for our trip to Paris."

"Your what?"

Mum's voice. She's stopped twisting the handle of the pasta machine. The sheet of fresh pasta falls pathetically onto the countertop. Philippe Dumont's hands, covered in mince and little bits of onion, are suspended mid-knead.

I'm not impressed. "Seriously, Mummy, have you forgotten already? I told you the other night! You know, when you were wearing that nipple-tastic blue nightgown! Astrid, Hakima and I are going to Paris."

"Are you now?" Mum asks, her nostrils flaring elegantly. "And when will this be?"

"Early July, once school's over."

"Oh yes? And how are you going to get there?"

"Mummy, Mummy, come on—you're the one who gave us the idea. We're going to cycle!"

As if to mimic our future pedalling, Mum starts turning the pasta machine's handle, slightly faster than a helicopter's rotor blades in mid-flight. Philippe Dumont begins kneading his mince again, his fingers emitting perfectly obscene sucking noises.

"How interesting," Mum says. "And how long is that going to take?"

"We haven't figured out everything yet, but we'll look it up online. There must be some website somewhere called How to Get from Bourg-en-Bresse to Paris by Bike.com."

"And where will you sleep?"

"Under the starry skies, or, should we encounter charitable strangers, on beds of hay in creaky barns."

"Perfect. And what are you going to do once you get there?"

The lasagne sheet splurging out of the pasta machine is now approximately the size of a shower curtain. "There in Paris, you mean, marvellous Mummy of mine?"

"That's what I mean, yes."

"Ah, Paris! The city of love. We'll just walk around, you know. Hang out in bars, drink tiny expensive espressos, eat macarons, all that stuff."

"Wonderful. And with what money?"

"With what money? Ha!"

Failing to come up with a plausible answer, I turn to Hakima and Astrid, who are being gradually ripped to shreds by an overexcited Fluffles. "Astrid! Stop feeding that cat your blood and tendons, we might need them. Tell my mother whence the money shall come for our Paris adventure."

Intense panic. Astrid stammers, "Well, we're going to... I mean, we'll..."

"We'll earn it!" suggests Hakima, raising her hand in the air.

Good start. "That's right," I confirm. "We'll earn the money."

"Earn it by doing what, exactly?" Mum asks sarcastically.

"Doing what? Well, that's what so funny about it. Tell her, Hakima."

"By... by doing... by finding..."

One correct answer a day being quite enough for our silver-medal piglette, she falls into confused silence.

But genius strikes elsewhere. "By *selling*!" Astrid yells.

"By selling," repeats Mum, still unrolling a Bayeux Tapestry-sized sheet of lasagne. "Very interesting. By selling what?"

"Come on, Mummy, isn't it obvious? By selling..."

"By selling..." says Astrid.

"By selling... plump..."

"...juicy..."

"...delicious..."

"...piggy..."

"..."

"...sausages!"

Philippe Dumont and Mum seem to have forgotten Mission Lasagne. "Plump juicy delicious piggy sausages," Mum echoes.

"Yes!" Astrid shouts. "We're going to sell sausages on the road!"

"Plain sausages, thyme sausages."

"And also vegetarian sausages for those who don't eat pork," adds Hakima. "Or else it's recrimination."

"Discrimination. Yes, exactly, Hakima, and we're not having any of that in our shop."

"No sir! Everyone welcome in our shop."

"Three types of sausage, three types of sauce," Astrid marvels. "Onion, mustard, apple! Fixed-price menu: one sausage, one sauce, three euros."

"Five euros," I correct. "Plus one drink, 6 euros."

"No, Mireille, we can't take drinks, it'll be too heavy," says Hakima. "Stick to the bare necessities."

"OK."

"She's right, it'll be too heavy for the trailer," says Astrid, on a roll.

"What trailer?" Mum groans.

"My mum's trailer," explains Astrid. "She uses it to wheel her pots around. I told you, Mireille—the one you can tow with a motorbike."

"You're going there by *motorbike*, now?"

"No, no," says Astrid, "we'll, erm... tweak it so it fits three bikes."

"Easy!" quoth I.

Philippe Dumont and Mum don't look like they think it's easy, or indeed sensible. Mum manages a remarkably calm, "Very well. We'll talk about it again later."

Philippe Dumont turns back to his mixing bowl of mince and onions, but I can tell his shoulders are shaking with something like laughter. A few minutes later he slips a scrunched-up Post-it note into my hand, on which he's scribbled Hélène Lesnout's phone number.

After dinner, once Astrid and Hakima have left, Mum sits me down at the kitchen table. I expect a full-on lecture on why there's absolutely no way she's letting us cycle through France on our own, with little Hakima who's much too young for us to be responsible for, and actually Astrid and I are much too young to be responsible for ourselves anyway, and bikes are dangerous because they go on roads, and the world is full of perverts who target young girls (even Pig Pageant winners), and you can't sell food without a hygiene certificate and a full eight-year training course validated by the Ministry of Food Trailers...

...and I've prepared answers to all these entirely unreasonable points; I'm ready to fight back with bullet-proof arguments, because in my blood runs that of Klaus Von Strudel, philosopher and logician.

But it turns out that's not what she wants to tell me.

What she wants to tell me, her cheeks gammon-pink, is much, much more unexpected.

"I have news, Mireille. Philippe and I are having a baby. Isn't that great?"

Something like a decade, or maybe even a full minute, ticks by. Time enough for Fluffles to pat a bit of mince off the table with his paw, poke it around the floor for a while, play ping-pong with it, eat it, spit it out, eat it again and suddenly run off up the stairs, terrified by what must be an aggressive-looking bit of fluff.

I haul my voice up from the depths of my throat. "A *baby*? What? Did you get IVF or something?"

Mum laughs, gets up and walks towards the stairs. "Why? Do you think we always sleep on opposite sides of the bed after a chaste kiss goodnight?"

"To my despair, I know for a fact you don't, but—I mean, you're not exactly young!"

"Thank you, you're such a darling. We're forty, it's not that old. Many people have children naturally at our age."

74

"Is it a boy or a girl?"

"What would you prefer?"

"Well, I already have three half-brothers, so I'd rather it was a girl."

"Tough luck, it's a boy."

"I hope he's less of a moron than his quarter-brothers. Oh, good Lord! I'm sure you're going to call him something idiotically posh, like Julius-Aurelian."

"We haven't yet picked a name, but thank you for offering to help."

"When's he scheduled for?"

"In five months."

"Five months! Why the rush? And what's going to happen to *me*? I'd happily be proven wrong, but I doubt he'll look like Jean-Paul Sartre, if you see what I mean. With a cocktail of your genes and Philippe Dumont's, he'll turn up looking already like a mini-Johnny Depp, and everyone will go, 'The Dumont-Laplanches, what a lovely family, with their new baby boy, Julius-Aurelian—such a cute little cherub, unlike that ugly duckling of a big sister, you know, that pig-faced—'"

"Mireille, you're giving me a headache."

"Will you go to school and teach with the baby hanging from your boob? Some mothers do that sometimes. It's atrocious. I refuse to condone such behaviour."

"I won't be teaching, since I'll be on maternity leave. And I don't know if I'll breastfeed. Is that all? Any other questions?"

"Yes. Why are you producing a *baby* instead of producing a major work of contemporary philosophy?"

She rolls her eyes, and oh! that sigh!

"No, but, Mum, listen—you've already got a daughter—I mean, I know it hasn't been an incredibly successful experiment, but you can cross that off the to-do list. Why have another baby now, when the real *you* is so crammed full of top-quality philosophy, just waiting to be unleashed on the world, Mummy, why, why..."

"I'm not a philosopher, Mireille," she snaps. "I'm just a philosophy teacher. Philosophers write philosophy books. Philosophy teachers read them and talk about them to their students. And occasionally, members of both categories are allowed to have children."

She walks up to her bedroom. And I finally *get* what it means to have *l'esprit de l'escalier*, when I scream to her, from the bottom of the staircase, "You know what? The ugliest thing Klaus gave you isn't even me. It's that idea that you're *just a philosophy teacher*."

Slam. The pregnant woman is going to bed.

Give her a break, I tell myself. Cells are dividing up inside her at this very minute. It must be tiring.

9

Astrid has asked her mum to lend us her trailer, and against all odds, the delightful lady has agreed, "in principle". She just wants to meet us first, to ensure that we are responsible and mature young women.

I think she must be a little crazy—what kind of mother of a sixteen-year-old girl assumes it *might* be OK for her daughter to cycle off across France selling sausages, with a twelve-year-old and a trailer in tow?

I ask Astrid, as she leads us through a charmingly overgrown garden towards her little country cottage, "Is your mum a little crazy? She doesn't mind us going off on our own?"

"No, she's not crazy, she's just... a bit of a hippy."

And so it seems she is. Laure Rosbourg, Astrid's mother, is exactly like her small, chalk-white, tumbledown house. Like her, the garden grows in every possible direction, healthily and chaotically, stuffed with snails and ladybirds. The house, like her, is stocky and short, capped with a roof of sun-bleached blonde slates. She's got potter's hands, with close-cropped nails. Every doorway is curtained with garlands of wooden beads. There are kitsch crucifixes everywhere on the walls, worm-eaten Bibles on the mismatched furniture, jostling for space with little plastic saints from Lourdes, and stone and resin statuettes brought back from trips abroad. On the fridge, under ugly magnets (Swiss dog with a barrel of brandy round its neck, Swiss flag, Swedish flag), Astrid smiles out at us from faded pictures: dressed as a scout; ready for communion; hiking in the Alps, her Germanic calves flashing under wide tan shorts. Most of the crockery is home-made, and the clay plates and cups are chunky and cracked, varnished, sometimes painted. Laure pours us some tea from the biggest, reddest teapot in the world.

"How lovely to meet Astrid's new friends," she says respectfully, as if we were adults like her. "I've heard so much about you. I'm glad Astrid's met some good, genuine people."

Are we good, genuine people? Hakima and I nod vigorously to make it look like we entirely agree with that definition.

"I think that the journey is an excellent idea. People today are much too afraid of letting children roam freely, sleep in the countryside and explore the world. But how about you, Hakima? Will your parents agree to let you go?"

"I haven't asked them yet," answers Hakima shyly. "I doubt they'll say yes."

I doubt it too, and that's very much the elephant in the room. How will we convince Hakima's parents? She's twelve and a half. At that age, you don't just cycle off to Paris from Bourg-en-Bresse, selling sausages, in the vague hope of gatecrashing a garden party at the presidential palace.

"You just need to tell them," says Laure, "that children used to wander around alone in forests and mountains all the time only a few generations ago. Some still do. Scouts, for instance."

"Exactly! But not scouts, we're expert sausage-sellers. We're punks! We're going to do our own thing. I'm sure your parents will say yes."

Not everyone's sure, though, and frankly, if I were Hakima's parents, I wouldn't let her go away with Mireille Laplanche and Astrid Blomvall: two single, childless only daughters, and also, incidentally, teenagers, ill-adapted to real life and wrapped in ill-fitting clothes, who only a few weeks back had absolutely no friends in the whole wide world.

And yet... you do end up being pretty good at taking care of people once you find a good reason for it. A good reason, such as, for instance, Hakima's little scrunched-up nose when she talks about the trip—and her black eyes, which suddenly seem to shine from the inside, as if lit up by two little LEDs.

Laure nods, and dishes out some hippy home-made biscuits—composed, as far as I can tell, of sugar, chocolate, butter, gravel and sand.

"I'll lend you the trailer," says Laure, opening the squeaky garage door. "Tweak it, repaint it, adapt it—I don't mind. May it bring you luck and joy. It's been with me a long time, and I spent the best months of my life with it, riding around selling pottery, before..."

Her voice breaks, as does a small clay pot that falls from a pile of boots and gardening supplies near the door.

"...before she had me and my father left her," concludes Astrid.

I picture Laure Rosbourg and her handsome Swedish boyfriend, towing the trailer through Europe, selling pots from town to town. A wandering life, not suited to the arrival of a podgy blonde baby with rheumy eyes. Is that why the Swedish man left? Is that why Astrid ended up in Switzerland, destined for a slightly dull but painless childhood with a soundtrack of Catholic hymns and Indochine songs?

The trailer is the size of a small car, with two large wheels. Two metal arms stretch out in front, meant to be hooked onto a motorbike. The right side of the trailer opens outwards and turns into a long shelf, which we'll use to sell the sausages. There's barely space for more than one of us inside, especially if we cram it with dishes and boxes full of sausages and sauces. The cracked paint on the outside still spells out the letters

RO B URG B OMVALL PO   RY

Laure finds an old piece of black slate on which to write our menu.

———

Next weekend, we'll give the trailer a makeover. In the meantime, we crash in Astrid's bedroom to plan the journey.

Well, I say "bedroom", but it's barely as big as the downstairs toilet in Mum and Philippe Dumont's mansion. The walls are entirely papered in Indochine posters, Indochine postcards and Indochine gig tickets, most of them black and white, making you feel like you've been buried alive in an old-fashioned Gothic horror film. Astrid seems to love her dungeon, though. Her huge laptop takes up all the available space on her small desk. We perch on the brown duvet.

"I looked up directions from Bourg-en-Bresse to the Élysée Palace on Google Maps," Astrid says, clicking a tab on her browser. "Here it is."

"Amazing," exclaims Hakima, "it's almost a straight line! And look, it's only four hours and ten minutes down the road!"

"Yeah, great," I say, "if you want to take all the motorways, and happen to be driving a car. I don't think we'll survive for long on three bikes with our sausage trailer. Astrid, dear, did you forget to click the bike icon, by any chance?"

"Maybe," admits Astrid.

She clicks said icon, tries to compute the journey again... and the computer crashes. The frozen screen refuses to give us an answer. A few Ctrl+Alt+Dels later, it seems clear that American supercomputers are unable to calculate the best cycling route from Bourg-en-Bresse to the Élysée Palace in Paris.

"I know," says Hakima, "you could type something like, 'How do you get to Paris from Bourg-en-Bresse by bike?' The Internet normally knows."

Indeed, it turns out that some Internet user asked a similar question five years ago on the forums of a website called "Francycle":

Raph01000

Hey everyone Id like to know the quickest route from Bourg-en-bresse to Paris by bike thanks!!

Some helpful answers follow:

MarcLapeyre

It would be much appreciated if you would ask a more precise question. How many days are you intending to spend on the road? Are you hoping to visit specific villages? What kind of bicycle do you own? In order for your question to be answered as effectively as possible, it is advisable to be precise (see forum rules on http://www.francycle.fr/forum/guidelinesforu...)

Raph01000

Hey sorry I mean like generally whats the quickest route. I just want to go to Paris from Bourg-en-bresse thats all I dont want to see villages lol

MarcLapeyre

Once again, your question lacks precision.

Clément1987

You should go through Burgundy following the wine road (http://www.francycle.fr/wineroa...) so you can taste the best ones while you're at it!!!! Enjoy!!! Clem87

Alaclaude1929

Don't forget to visit Cluny on the way. There are beautiful villages that have won awards for their parks and gardens. You will find a full listing here (http://www.francesmostbeautifulvilla...). I would recommend a lovely little restaurant in Thoissey where they serve delicious frogs' legs in cream—though we last went there a few years ago and it might have closed down since.

Raph01000

No but I dont care about gardens frogs legs wine and all that!? it's just that the train is expensive so can someone just tell me how to go to Paris by bike!!

MarcLapeyre

You are on a forum used by people who are passionate about cycling and about the French countryside; this is not eBay. Here, we care about landscape and healthy exercise, not about saving money. If you have never cycled this far before, you might strain yourself physically. Here is some advice http://www.francycle.fr/training/physicalprepar...

Moderator

Raph01000, you can just use the free mapping tool provided to Francycle users: http://www.francycle.fr/planyourtrip...

Raph01000

Christ! finally!!!!! thanks thats exactly the kind of thing I was after

Solved—Topic closed

Solved indeed! The magic tool allows us to plan our route according to all the criteria we want—maximum number of days on the road, stopovers in villages or towns...

"...with potential sausage-buyers..."

"Not sure they've got that option," says Astrid.

...bike shops on the way, type of road, etc. Some bits of the route are also visible on pictures. We spot little paths alongside fields, hawks perched on fences, Romanesque churches, cyclists and swathes of blue sky.

Finally, the complete route comes up: six days, five nights, given five to seven hours of pedalling each day. The bright-red route snakes up the map of France, going through South Burgundy, then alongside the River Loire, all the way up to the south of Paris. If we leave Bourg-en-Bresse on 8th July at 2 p.m., we'll be at the Élysée Palace on 14th July at midday.

We stare at that red line and imagine all it represents: open fields, quaint villages, riverbank paths and potential sausage-eaters... and we go silent, very silent, so silent we can hear the drum roll of our three impatient, happy hearts.

A chequered black-and-white flag ("Destination") is planted on Saint-Honoré Street, on the north bank of the River Seine in Paris. It symbolizes the scandalous revelation that Klaus is my father, Indochine's concert, and General Sassin's public shaming.

I squeeze my two piglettes in an almighty hug. It's nice to have two plump juicy friends to hug; like hugging two human-sized Fluffleses, warm, padded and purring.

"Mireille, you're strangling me." (Hakima)

"Me too." (Astrid)

"I'm so excited!"

"We've still got a lot of preparing to do."

"And parents to convince," Hakima says.

"We'll do it. We'll do it. We'll manage it. We'll get there—to the black-and-white flag—we'll get there on 14th July at midday! We will. We *will*!"

10

"Y ou will *not*."

Hakima's parents are not keen.

"Are you out of your mind? Of course you're not going on that trip." Hakima's mum says a few things in Arabic, to which Hakima replies, also in Arabic. Then, back to French: "No, Hakima, they're *fifteen*! You're not a *responsible adult* at fifteen!"

I am minded to object that you can be a hugely responsible adult at fifteen, that I am actually fifteen and a half, and Astrid sixteen, which is the age of all Disney princesses when they get married. My legendary debating skills, however, are currently catatonic, because the Sun is here among us, throwing dark, regal glances at Astrid and me. He's looking intrigued, and his furrowed brow seems to spell out a perplexed question: *Why are these plump little piglettes building such castles in the sky?*

"But it'll be the three of us together!" Hakima implores. "We won't split up, I promise, *[Arabic word]*, we'll stay together, we—"

"Hakima: no."

"I've never seen Paris!"

"We'll take you, if it means so much to you! What's all this craziness about? There's absolutely no need to—"

"There *is*!" Hakima yells. "There *is* a need! We *have* to prevent that murderer Sassin from getting his medal! We *have* to rip it off his chest!"

Silence. The Sun sits up.

Hakima's parents wait for him to speak, uncertain how to react.

He speaks. Softly.

"Hakima... it's not your duty to *avenge* me, you know."

His *avenge* in italics whips through the air.

"Why not, Kader?... Why not? You're not going to do it yourself, I can tell. You're not doing anything at all! You stay here all day long in your chair, sulking."

"Things have become a bit more difficult recently," the Sun whispers. "As you may have noticed."

"You used to drive tanks through the desert. That was difficult too."

The Sun's jaw tightens. "We'll do something once we hear back from the internal inquiry. Then we'll know. Then we'll be able to do something—"

"The inquiry won't lead anywhere, and you know it!" Hakima sobs. "You've always said it! I don't even understand why you keep going on and on about that inquiry, while saying all the time that it won't lead anywhere! At least we'll *do* something, if we gatecrash that garden party."

"Hakima," her father interjects, "what does gatecrash even *mean*? What sort of word is that? And what's with all these crazy ideas? Cycling, sausages, the—the *garden party*. What kind of nonsense is this?"

The Sun, meanwhile, is lost in thought. Hakima stares at him, as if he alone could convince his parents.

And apparently, he can.

"She's right," he says slowly. "Maybe we do need to do something like that if we want to get anywhere. It's true, we keep repeating that the internal inquiry will lead nowhere—that it'll never do justice to us and to the other soldiers, because we're immigrants, who live far away from Paris. Maybe... maybe we do need to do something... spectacular."

"*Kader!*" His mother's voice, like an arrow—that misses its target. She knows she's already lost.

"Listen," he says. "What if... what if I went with them? If I'm there it'll be simpler for everyone. I'll look after Hakima, Mum. I'll go to Paris with them. I'll get into the Élysée Palace with them if they can do it. And maybe at last *something* will happen."

"You can't be responsible for three young girls," his father mutters.

"Do you think it's that much more difficult than being responsible for ten soldiers?" the Sun laughs.

Then he sort of gulps back a sob... which leaves a bitter taste in his mouth, judging by the look on his face. "Yeah, I guess you're right. Those soldiers I was responsible for all got killed."

The deepest silence. Madame Idriss glowers at her husband.

"Don't be silly, Kader. Of course you're perfectly able to look after these three girls."

A lucky blow—or a carefully aimed karate chop?—Kader's father's little gaffe forces them to grant us their blessing. They're far from happy about it, of course. But they know that for the past year the Sun's been a prisoner: of his own body, of their apartment, of Bourg-en-Bresse. They can see he's become pale and sickly, this man who used to be so full of life and energy. This man who used to swim through swamps and climb up mountains, and who has had to spend months with a nurse, relearning how to wash himself. This man who used to run for miles every day, and who suddenly found it a struggle to go from the sofa to the wheelchair and from the wheelchair to the bed.

All this I know from Hakima—not that she said much. During all those weeks, those months, he never cried once, but often, burning with rage, he rolled himself up into a ball on the rug, and burst into dark solar storms.

"So that's settled, then," the Sun says. "I'll go with them."

So that's settled. The thought of spending six days and five nights beaded with drops of sweat next to the Sun fills me with terror and ecstasy.

"Just one thing, though," Astrid says, shyly.

"Yes, what?"

"How are you going to... you know? How are you going to—like—*cycle*?"

"Oh, *that*," says the Sun.

And suddenly he's truly beaming. "*That* will be my chance to test a certain little thing that was delivered to my friend Jamal a few weeks ago."

You know what? I think the Sun has been *waiting* for an opportunity like this to come along.

He has been waiting for something to get him back into action; for an excuse to do something. Recently, it's almost as if he's been preparing for it—lifting weights every day, alone, stubbornly; doing ten pull-ups, a hundred, a thousand, on the bar wedged in his bedroom doorway.

His friends have got the message: Kader is dreaming again, of sports, adventure, open roads. So all of them— Jamal, Thomas, Zach, Pedro and little Soliman, and Anissa who was going out with Jamal but a little bit in love with Kader, have pulled their money together to buy him...

"Oh, *wow*."

The gleaming machine seems to illuminate Jamal's dark bedroom. It's made of extra-light aluminium and fibreglass; it's got two huge slanted wheels, turned slightly inwards, and a padded seat. The Ferrari of wheelchairs. At last, a heavenly chariot worthy of such a Sun God.

"The model those Paralympics guys use," Jamal points out.

The Sun's eyes, like two little silver mirrors, reflect the shiny wheelchair.

"I can't believe you managed to convince him!" smiles Anissa, a supple young woman, draped over Jamal's desk chair. "We've been trying for over a month!"

"I was always going to give in," the Sun sighs. "I know it cost you—"

"...an arm and a leg," Jamal scoffs. "Lucky you didn't buy it yourself—there wouldn't be much of you left."

The Sun flicks him the finger, neatly demonstrating how he would still find a use for that last remaining arm. Then, like a hermit crab leaving its shell for another one, he squeezes out of his old wheelchair, and pops into the Paralympics fibreglass space machine.

Jamal flings open the bedroom door, which leads to the garage.

And then... then the Sun meets the chair meets the street, in a long scream of joy.

It's almost like he's flying, his ultra-light racing machine ricocheting from pavement to pavement. Barely two minutes, and he's already one with it. His biceps tense as he grasps the wheels (which I observe purely out of intellectual curiosity, of course), and then his triceps bulge as he propels himself forward (an interesting physical phenomenon); it looks very much like his abs might be contracting under his T-shirt as he performs swift half-turns (but we can't be sure, since he isn't topless).

Soon, the Sun's having fun, starts to boast, to sprint, to twist—he even tries to swing onto one wheel, falls heavily to the side when trying a hairpin turn, but a moment later he's back on his feet—well, wheels—and laughs, and shouts, and we're all laughing and shouting with him.

Except for Hakima, who's sobbing so hard she's got no breath left for laughter.

Still buzzing from all that energy, we're more than ready to get started learning the best way to cook home-made sausages.

II

The Georges & Georgette has two Michelin stars and an average of 4.89 stars out of five on TripAdvisor, where such comments as the following may be found:

> Traditional cuisine of the Bresse region. Magical! Picturesque views of the church of Brou. Amazing oven-cooked quenelles. We'll be back!

> We had a lovley time at the Georges & Georgette. Delicious, traditoinal French food—we were tempted by the frogs but opted for a safer choice, the bouef borgignon, which was divine. Warm and wecloming.

> Lovely restaurant managed by lovely people. A legendary Bourg-en-Bresse restaurant!

> Don't be fooled by the traditional look of this splendid inn located right opposite the church of Brou. Freshly redecorated, elegant, sophisticated, but also friendly, the restaurant serves dishes that are traditional only in name. Each one is a rediscovery—a new twist on food, a new metaphysical vision of the ingredients you

think you know. From the veal blanquette to the crème caramel, you will never cease to be surprised by the delights of the Georges & Georgette. A couple of lovely little touches complete the experience: home-made butter and bread; perfect matching of wine to food thanks to the restaurant sommelier. A family-run restaurant of stupefying standard at the heart of the Bresse.

[OK, I'm the one who wrote that last one, under the pseudonym JeanLouisFrom01]

Of course, there are also those who disagree:

it was rubbish

Thank you, very constructive criticism. Also, inevitably:

The food is not exactly what you would call healthy. Don't hope to find a light salad on the menu.

My wife's gluten allergy proved impossible to accommodate.

Since my grandparents don't have a clue how to go onto TripAdvisor, they don't care. They're grumpy, irascible, gluttonous and stubborn; they're tough with their employees (often) and their customers (occasionally); apart from that, they're charming people. This Friday night after school and before the restaurant opens, they welcome us into their huge kitchen. Hakima whispers, "Wow! It's like we're in *Ratatouille*!"

Grandad flashes his famous dimply smile. "So you want to learn to make sausages?"

"Only vegetarian ones—the other ones we'll order from Raymond. Oh, and we also need you to teach us to make some sauces."

"And to package it all in a light and convenient way," says Astrid, her strategic brain-cogs whirring.

"Vegetarian sausages? You mean, with chicken?"

"No, Grandad, vegetarian, as in: without meat."

"With fish?"

"No, nothing from any animal."

"What kind of newfangled invention is that? We'll need some guts to keep it all together!"

My grandmother: "Shush, Georges, we can do it without the guts! It'll stick together, if we find the right mix."

Grandad grumbles, declares that it's the silliest thing he's ever heard, and don't count on him to even touch that vegetarian sausage; he'll just give us his recipe for mustard sauce, and believe me, no one will want your dirty vegetarian sausage!

"Let's see," says my grandmother soothingly. "We could have a mixture of breadcrumbs with, for instance, leeks, goats' cheese, chives..."

She mixes, blends, rolls, weighs, fries; meanwhile, Astrid is delighted because the situation is "virtually indistinguishable" from *Kitchen Rush*—as she enthusiastically explains to my grandfather, it's a video game where you have to manage a restaurant but there's salmonella, health-and-safety inspectors, unhappy customers...

Grandad nods and nods: ohhhh yes, he knows about *that* all right. But at some point Astrid says, "There're also out-of-date ingredients you absolutely can't forget to throw away, or else—"

"WHAT?! There'll be none of *that* talk round here, young lady!"

He swings his big knife right beneath her nose.

"We don't throw away *anything* in this kitchen! We've got tins of goose fat from 1956!"

"And it's still perfectly good!" Grandma confirms vigorously.

"Absolutely! Goose fat doesn't go out of date."

"Nor does crème fraiche!"

"In *Kitchen Rush*," says Astrid, "it does."

"Hrrrmph! Your electronic gizmos go out of date faster than my crème fraiche," Grandad grumbles. "Right, you want to learn to make that sauce, or what? To work!"

So we learn to make vegetarian sausages, mustard sauce and onion sauce, while dodging my grandparents' long knives and wooden spoons. The assistant chefs begin to trickle in for tonight's first service, and are asked to join in.

"Here, Jean-Pierre, have a bite of that vegetarian sausage. What do you think?"

"Not enough meat."

"Right, but apart from that?"

"Apart from that, it's very nice."

We even serve some slices of the sausage as an *amuse-bouche* to the first diner of the evening—an accountant, famous in the region, who's making the most of her dinner partner's lateness to read through an important file.

We are all tense as we wait for her verdict, huddled like spies at the kitchen door...

The blonde accountant puts down her BlackBerry for a minute, chews a bit of vegetarian sausage dipped in onion sauce... asks to talk to the chef...

"She said it was delicious!" Grandma tells us on the way back.

A round of applause, and Grandad rushes to serve the accountant a large glass of some local red wine.

"And now," Grandma begins, "the apple compote..."

"No!" shouts Astrid. "*I* know how to make apple compote!"

"Really?"

Our blonde half-Swede falters, noticing the suspicious glances my grandparents shoot each other.

"Yes," she stammers, "I was always on compote duty at the convent..."

(Oh, what fun one must have at that convent.)

"How do you make it, then?"

"It's my thing, I know exactly..."

"Well, *tell us*, then, young lady!"

The Adam's apple of the young lady bobs up and down a little. After a sufficient amount of anxious swallowing, she stutters, "You take the apples..."

"What kind?"

"B... Bos... Boskoop?..."

They nod.

"You... youp... youp—*peel*—them?"

Another nod.

"You take the pips out?"

Nod, nod.

"And then?" asks my grandmother slyly. "You get a big pan out, and pour a small amount of water into it?... Don't you?..."

Complete silence. Everyone, including all the assistant chefs, is staring at Astrid.

Sling, sling, goes my grandfather's knife on the sharpening rod.

Pssshroooof! goes a blowtorch that my grandmother has inexplicably produced from a drawer.

"Nnnnno," whispers Astrid. "Well, maybe *you* do, but I—in my version, I..."

The blue flame purrs, the knife sings...

"...I put them in the oven for ten minutes first, so they taste a little bit smoky."

"COME TO MY ARMS, DEAR CHILD!" my grandparents shout in perfect harmony, and a general hugging session follows.

While everyone's congratulating everyone else, Hakima and I stuff our faces with vegetarian sausages dipped in the two sauces.

"Like it?"

Her mouth full, Hakima stretches out her podgy little thumb.

The trailer's makeover takes the whole weekend.

At first, Philippe Dumont isn't all that pleased to hear we'll be flinging paint and polish all over his driveway, and coating his beautiful lawn with wood and steel shavings from all the hammering, drilling, filing, soldering and scraping. But he lets us do it.

The Sun and Jamal are there to help (which they do mostly by bringing us bags of Haribo). Philippe Dumont's toolbox has never been used so much in its life, and its limitations are soon keenly felt. The neighbour lends us his much bigger box, taking pity on Astrid, whose efforts with the minuscule drill aren't going anywhere, and on Hakima, who's trying to repaint a huge board with a brush more suitable for eggshell decoration.

It's a well-organized operation. First, we tweak the trailer so our three bikes can tow it. For that purpose, we buy three half-bikes for children—the kind that clip onto an adult bike and only have one wheel—from a local bike shop. We chuck away the single wheels, and replace them with a hollow aluminium bar, which we then fix to two solid chains linked to the trailer.

We clip the transformed children's bikes to ours, we jump on, and we're off!

And, beautifully, we fall flat on our faces, to howls of laughter from the Sun and Jamal.

We get back in the saddle and keep trying until we get it right: we have to pedal at the same rhythm, or else the metal bar gets pulled forward on one side and not the other, and everyone ends up on the floor.

Gradually, we learn each other's pedalling tempos: Hakima's vivacious, irregular pushes; Astrid's long strokes, powered by her scout-like endurance; my own oscillating enthusiasm, alternating three minutes of energetic speed with three minutes of intense muscle fatigue.

Then we have to decorate the trailer. Hakima the artist cuts out stencils from discarded board; letters (S, A, U, G and E to make SAUSAGES, and T, H, R, P, I, G and L to make THE THREE LITTLE PIGLETTES), and also animals, flowers and fruit—birds, tulips, fish, pigs, carrots, apples—which we stick to the sides of the trailer and drench with colourful spray paint that we found in Jamal's bedroom ("How funny that you've got all this spray paint in your house, Jamal!" pipes the touchingly naive Hakima.)

After all our work, believe me, that trailer looks good. It's like something from one of those TV makeover programmes. Not the most tastefully decorated of trailers, perhaps, but it's eye-catching enough. One thing's for sure: that silver cube, with its colourful patterns, towed by three mismatched bikes ridden by three little piglettes, and the Sun in his chariot out in front—you'll be able to see it coming from a mile away!

And hear it, and smell it! Once the smell of paint gets replaced by that of our sausages, sizzling away in the pans... and the bubbling compote, and the caramelized onions, curling sensuously up on themselves like woodlice—and the peppery mustard, softened by the cream...

"I don't understand why you insist on calling your-selves the Three Little Piglettes," Mum groans. "It's a horrible name."

"We'll make it beautiful, you'll see. Or better, we'll make it powerful."

Auntie Mireille's Life Tips: take whatever insults they throw at you and knit them into a lovely big hat.

It's a beautiful Sunday night, still warm at 10 p.m. We wolf down pizzas, admiring our masterpiece, incongru-ously parked here on the posh lawn; the dog Kittycat steals entire slices of our pizza; the cat Fluffles leaps like a flea to catch the moths knocking themselves out on the globular garden lamps.

Life's pretty flawless, right now, out here under the stars.

To crown it all, the Sun's speaking to me.

"What will you tell your biological dad, when you see him?"

"I don't know yet. I'll introduce myself first, I guess. Put him on the spot. See the fear on his face when he realizes I'm the one who sent him those letters."

"And then?"

"Then, I don't know, I'll play it by ear."

"If I were him, I'd be very happy to be your father."

I frown. "You're not old enough to be my father!"

"Then why do you talk to me in that voice?"

"What voice?"

"All respectful and shy, like I'm your teacher or some-thing. Relax, I'm not going to eat you."

Which is a shame, seeing how much he seems to be enjoying his calzone. I catch a moth just to annoy Fluffles, who's been pawing at it for a while. The unhappy insect flutters between my fingers.

Fluffles pats my fist, hoping I'll let him have it.

"No problem. I'll relax. I'll stop hoping you're going to eat me. I mean, stop worrying you might."

"Cool."

"How about you? What will you tell Sassin?"

The Sun smiles to the moon. "I'll play it by ear."

One week of school left, and then, two weeks later, we're away.

One important last thing before we go, though: training.

12

"**H**ey, Miss Piggy! Is it true what people say? You're getting up at 5 a.m. these days to cycle through the forest of Seillon?"

Cornered in the arts corridor, just before the last lesson of the year.

"Hey, Babes, what's up?"

"Don't call me Babes. Who do you think you are? Bitch!"

It is not pleasant to be surrounded by Malo and his sidekicks, big Rémi (whose dopey giggles reek of weed) and tiny Marvin, who has acquired Nike platform trainers in the hope of looking taller, and beach-ball-sized biceps in the hope of diverting attention from his girlishly slender frame.

"Not keen to be a pig any more, are you? Finally decided to become a real woman? It feels good, you'll see."

Rémi's dopey giggle. Me: "Sounds like you know what you're talking about. When did you become a real woman?"

Rémi's dopey giggle. Malo: "Shut up. What are you and the other fuglies up to?"

"What do you mean, Babes?"

"Walid saw you in Seillon cycling along like a load of fat sows."

"Oh, has he seen fat sows cycling before, then? Interesting."

"Shut up. Why are you cycling?"

The bell rings, and Madame Karandash's frizzy head pops out of the arts classroom to rally her troops.

"Aren't we allowed to? This is a free country."

"Don't mess me around. I got a call from Hélène Lesnout. She wants me to respond to something for an article she's writing."

"Hélène who?"

He's not joking about not messing him around; he pushes me against the wall with, I have to admit, surprising strength.

"That journalist bitch. You got in touch with her to say you were up to something, something about pigs. Shut up! I'm talking. She said you were onto something big. That you were going to get revenge, or something. No, shut your mouth! I'm talking. Listen, I don't know what you're hoping to do, but if you're trying to mess with me because of that pageant thing, if you're trying to—to make me look bad or something, if you're—I'll smash your fucking heads in, you hear me? I'll rip your fat pigs' heads off. I'll gut you, understand?"

"Malo, Rémi, Marvin, it's time for class! You too, Mireille! Just because it's the last day of school doesn't mean being late is OK."

104

He drops me.

My knees feel a little weak. But after all, for the past three days I've woken up at five to go cycling for two hours in the forest of Seillon before school. And every evening, another two hours.

No wonder my joints are a bit sore.

That evening, I call Hélène Lesnout. "What's wrong with you? When you're writing an article about us, you don't even bother to ask for our opinion—and for this one, you run straight to Malo?"

"You hadn't told me not to."

"I thought it was obvious! Don't do it again, or we'll never tell you why we're doing all this."

"Isn't it just to get back at Malo?"

"No, it's got nothing to do with him. It's much cooler than that. Just keep following us, and you'll see."

"Can't you just tell me now?"

"No. Each day, we'll tell you a little more. And on 14th July, you'll know everything."

Hélène Lesnout is hooked. For now, all she knows is that we're planning a cycle ride from Bourg-en-Bresse to Paris, selling sausages as we go. But whatever for? And what will we do once we get there? We're keeping it a secret.

But the *Bresse Courier* newspaper isn't against that kind of secrecy. It whets the readers' appetites. The first article will be published on the day we leave, namely, on the morning of 8th July.

In the meantime, we train, train, train. Every morning, every evening.

"Why, Mireille!" Ms Lyse, our PE teacher, marvels. "You're running around like a little mountain goat today!"

"I must be on a high because the holidays are coming soon."

"I see... Shame I had to wait for the very last lesson of the year to witness that budding sprinting talent."

"Do you think I could beat Usain Bolt, Ms Lyse?"

"I wouldn't bet all my savings on it, but *what's for sure*," she says, louder, "*is that you'll easily beat Malo and his little friends, if they keep up that sluggish pace for the whole class...*"

Hearing that mighty threat, Malo glares at me and darts off at top speed along the track.

"Yeah but, Ms Lyse," Rémi guffaws, "she's cheating, Mireille, Ms Lyse, she's cheating, cos she goes cycling every morning in the forest of Seillon!" (dopey giggle).

"I don't call that cheating, I call that healthy living," Ms Lyse answers. "If I were you, Rémi, I'd go with her, instead of smoking outside the school gate at eight in the morning..."

Energized by these wise words, I run around the track another three or four times. Some people laugh at me. I don't care: they're scoffing and sweating and I'm soaring. Soaring!

Then it's time to leave for "a well-deserved summer rest", as the head says. Tears, sobs, hugs.

Or, in my case, just a quick *bye!* to the school walls before meeting up with Hakima and Astrid right outside. No time for kissing the losers inside—we've got five miles of forest paths to cycle. And then another hour with the trailer in tow. That trailer is so heavy. Pulling it makes us sweat like cheeses under a cloche.

And then those showers! Freezing, astonishingly generous—drenching our broken bodies, our burning joints, our blood-red faces. After that, huge plates of pasta, rice salad, cheese and ham quiches. And at last, sleep—a sleep so deep, every night, that even Fluffles's claws (the idiot regularly mistakes my toes for mice) don't wake me up.

One week of that routine, then another.

Then there's only a few days left, and then only a few hours, before it's time to go.

13

"You can't go. You're not even allowed to sell food! You'll poison everyone..."

"Don't worry, Mummy darling, we'll keep it cold and follow the three-second rule."

"Keep it cold how? That little fridge's only got enough battery for six days!"

"It's chargeable."

"You'll get stopped by the cops before you're more than a couple of streets away."

"We'll cycle too fast for them to catch us."

"Seriously, Mireille: your journalist friend wants to write a feature on your little trip, and you don't think the police might be a bit intrigued? Don't count on me to pick you up from the Bourg-en-Bresse police station."

I sigh deeply, and slip something out of my pocket: a licence to sell food from a trailer, in the name of Kader Idriss. Mum's speechless (for at least two seconds).

"And you think the cops will be happy with your Kader getting underage girls to work for him?"

"He's not my Kader. Mum, are you helping us or what? You're such a wet blanket sometimes!"

She emits a few irritated groans and starts helping us load the trailer. Since she's currently full of that little bastard Brad Pitt Junior, aka Julius-Aurelian, she can only carry light things; Philippe Dumont and Astrid, meanwhile, are offloading trays of sausages from Raymond's van. Hakima's parents are talking to Kader very fast, doubtlessly in the hope of talking him out of the trip. No chance. Astrid's mother is admiring our tweaks to her trailer.

Pots of sauce and tubs of compote have been Tetrised around the mini fridge, the portable hobs and the small gas bottle we'll need to top up on the way. There're also two extra-light easy-opening tents in there, carefully folded. And plenty of spare pairs of pants; the other clothes will be washed and dried along the way if need be.

"You've got a full list of the campsites you'll be stopping at?"

"Of course!" (not.)

"Phone charger?"

(She's bought us a solar panel that we've screwed to the roof of the trailer. It's so sunny that it's currently producing much too much electricity, and is possibly at risk of exploding.)

"Fluffles, get out of that trailer! You're not coming with us!"

"What's the time?" Astrid asks.

"Eight fifteen. We've got to go. We're already a quarter of an hour late."

"Your helmets!"

"*Yes*, Mum, chill out, we won't forget."

We strap them on; so does the Sun, in his wheelchair.

Hakima's parents, Mum and Philippe Dumont are infinitely perplexed.

Wait a second... Who's that lurking in the bushes? Might it be Malo, looking rather twitchy, in his silly Arsenal T-shirt? Relax, Babes, where's your swagger now?

Hélène Lesnout takes a picture for tomorrow's article. Flash!

Astrid's mother snaps a Polaroid. Click! Whirrr. There'll be no time for us to wait for it to dry.

I'm in the middle, on my blue Bicycool. I turn to Astrid, on my left.

"Ready?"

"Ready."

To Hakima, on my right.

"Ready?"

"Ready."

And, finally, I call out to the Sun, in front of us.

"Ready, Kader?"

"Ready, *bella*."

Bella? Seems like I'm solar-powered today too. My first pedal stroke makes the earth spin beneath my wheel!

"We're off!"

PART II

The Road

A TRIP WITH "THREE LITTLE PIGLETTES"

They were voted the ugly ducklings of their high school—now they're flying like swans to Paris. Astrid Blomvall, Hakima Idriss and Mireille Laplanche, the winning trio of a controversial "pig pageant", are embarking on what promises to be an epic journey to the capital ... by bike! Scheduled to last from 8th to 14th July, the journey will be funded, ironically, by selling pork sausages en route.

But why are they going to Paris? The three young ladies, for now, are keeping the goal of their journey a secret. "There's something that links us all to each other," confides Laplanche, "and that something can only be found in Paris on 14th July."

The self-proclaimed "Three Little Piglettes" will be escorted by Hakima's older brother Kader Idriss, 26. The young man is the only survivor of the massacre of [El-Khatastrophi] in [Problemistan]. A double amputee, he will be making the journey in a wheelchair.

H.L.

Comments, questions? Join the conversation on TheBresseCourier.fr, where we'll be following the "Three Little Piglettes" over the next six days.

("What, you mean we're not going to be featured in the paper edition every day?"

"Are you joking, my dear? We'll update the website, that's quite enough, and we'll see how people react. Three girls on bikes—not exactly the year's biggest scoop."

"Not *yet*.")

14

The first morning is uneventful—it's too early for potential readers of the *Bresse Courier* to have bought and read it, so we leave Bourg-en-Bresse with no curious glances whatsoever. We are calm, focused. My eyes switch from the road to my hands to the small GPS strapped to my handlebars. In front of me, the Sun leads the way. From where I'm sitting, I can only see the back of his head and his arms, like pistons, rhythmically pushing the wheelchair's tyres onwards.

Behind us, the trailer bounces over potholes, skids on gravel and grit, and groans loudly whenever we slow down. We have to be careful—if we brake too sharply, the trailer will run straight over us. We can't go down any too-steep slopes—it'd go down faster than us and, again—splat. We knew the risks, so we've planned our route to avoid hills.

We stay quiet, determined, eating up mile after mile, no rush. Three and a quarter hours later, we've cycled twenty-two miles. Seven miles an hour, for three little piglettes dragging a trailer—not too shabby, eh? I'd like to see you try.

The twenty-two miles have taken us to Mâcon, where we stop for our very first sausage-selling experience.

"How's it going, Kader?" Astrid asks the Sun, who's currently stretching in his chair.

It baffles me that she can speak to him without turning fuchsia, without stammering, without swinging stupidly on one leg while scratching her head in an extremely awkward manner.

"All right. How about you? Not in pain?"

"Nope! I'm good."

"How about you, Mireille?"

Mireille, the Sun's asking you a question. Give him a cool, detached reply.

"I'm good, thanks. Just a bit sore between the legs, but nothing out of the ordinary."

Wait, what? *Just a bit sore between the legs?* For God's sake, you've just talked to the Sun about your groin. *Nothing out of the ordinary?* He's going to think you've got an ugly case of gonorrhoea. To hide my horror, I rush to the trailer.

"Right—shall we open that sausage shop?"

Mâcon, in case you've never been, is a nice, big, red-and-ochre city, its feet dipped in the river Saône, over which a large stone bridge has been built. Many meandering streets lead to a couple of churches, giving occasional indications of the city's tortuous history.

All these details, I hope, are of no interest whatsoever to you, because this isn't a travel guide. We're here for work, I'll have you know. I've been to Mâcon before, though—with my artificial daddy Philippe Dumont, who is Rotary buddies with a certain Monsieur Tanincourt, a local wine merchant.

"You see, Mireille, that's how you choose wine—do you notice the lighter shade at the top? It means—"

"Philippe Dumont, you're driving us back, remember. How many glasses have you had so far?"

"Mimi darling! Would I bring you back to your mother in more than one piece?"

"You will if you keep swigging down everything Monsieur Tanincourt brings you to taste."

"Children are such tyrants! Mireille dear, I'm trying to teach you things... important things... why do you never listen to me? I'd so like—*hic*—to hand down my knowledge to the next geren—gena—generation..."

But not today. Today, on Lamartine square, near the grey-green waters of the Saône, we open up shop.

The Sun to his sister: "Do you know about Lamartine, Hakima?"

"Oh, yeah. Isn't he the husband of one of the Kardashians?"

"No, that's Lamar Odom..."

Back in the trailer, our expert chef Astrid is already popping open all the sauce tins. She gets out two pans, plonks them on the portable hobs, and starts heating up a bit of sunflower oil. For the first time, I start to feel sick: dry mouth, shaky fingers. What if they hate our sausages? What if they laugh at us? What if they all drop dead from food poisoning?

"Sausages! Nice plump juicy sausages! Plain! Thyme! Vegetarian!" the Sun shouts, and Hakima echoes (more quietly) to the passers-by.

"One sausage, one sauce, three euros!"

It's lunchtime, and the smell of frying sausages—and the sight of their warm caramel-coloured curves in the pans—should seduce all human beings in the vicinity into forcing upon us all their worldly goods, in the hope of tasting our wares.

However, that does not happen.

Weird.

Half an hour ticks by. We're all a little hungry, so we get sandwiches from a shabby cafe. We're all a little thirsty, so we crack open a couple of Coke cans in our trailer. Stress levels begin to rise.

Yet people *are* stopping; they sniff the air loaded with the smell of cooking meat and vegetables; they throw a glance at the apple compote, at the wholegrain-mustard sauce...

...and then they see Hakima and the Sun.

I cough. "I have a feeling you're putting them off," I whisper.

"Funny that," says the Sun. "I have exactly the same impression."

"Why would we be putting them off?" asks little Hakima. "Cos we're ugly?"

"Kader isn't ugly!" I protest. "And, erm, you aren't either."

"Is it because Kader doesn't have any legs, then?" asks Hakima sadly.

"Yeah, maybe," the Sun mutters. "Listen, Hakima, let's be the chefs, all right? Mireille and Astrid can sell the food."

So we swap. And miraculously, it works.

It's not that people are racist, you know. It's just that they'd rather talk to two ugly white girls than to a *tanned* handsome man. I've got a hunch it'll be the same everywhere. Wait, can I say *a hunch* when there's a disabled man in this convoy? I'm hyper-aware of my vocabulary all of a sudden—so many things to think about.

Anyway, ten minutes later, a sizeable crowd has gathered at our trailer.

"Hey, wait a minute—aren't you the girls they talked about in the paper this morning?"

"Yes, sir! That would be us! What sauce would you like?"

"Mustard! What are they on about, calling you pigs? You're a lovely bunch of ladies! I'd be proud to call you my... erm..."

"Daughters?"

"Well, let's say nieces. Thank you very much!"

He runs off and shouts to his wife, "I've just bought sausages from those kids, you know, the three ugly girls they talked about in the paper? They're over there!"

Some time ago, that would have hurt, but now we're just finding it funny, and the euros tinkle in the piggy bank.

"Can I get a picture with you, girls?"

"Of course!"

Flash! Flash! For every selfie, a sausage sold. A little worried, the Sun checks his phone sporadically, making sure we're not being slammed on social media. But no, it could be worse.

Florent Rooster @florentrooster
#selfie with #3littlepiglettes in Mâcon! Delicious apple/onion mix
Retweeted by @bressecourier   5 likes

Hugo Nallay @gohunal
Sausages on the banks of the Saone with my love <3
#3littlepiglettes
Retweeted by @sarah01   1 like

Jacques Creuz @jacquescreuz
Lunch break after triathlon practice to taste sausages from #3littlepiglettes. They'll be in Cluny tonight—catch them if u can

An hour later, the *Bresse Courier* has already stolen the pictures taken by passers-by, and we've got our own little news story:

Bresse Courier @bressecourier
#3littlepiglettes have reached Mâcon for their very first sale http://www.bressec...

"Don't read the comments," says the Sun.

I do anyway. The first ten are all variations on the theme of WHAT FUCKING DOGS and WHOD EAT SAUSAGE

THATS MADE BY THERE HANDS I SWEAR THEY DONT
WASH THEMSELVES THOSE DIRTY SOWS

I wonder what sort of people could be writing comments like that. Certainly not the same ones who are here, buying sausages from us.

"Shouldn't we make sure we don't sell everything?" Hakima worries.

"Yeah, we should be getting a move on. Another couple of sales, and let's go. The road awaits! And Cluny this evening…"

"Hey, Mireille, look at that statue over there!"

"It's Lamartine, Hakima."

"Oh, that's him. What's his story?"

"He was a poet."

"What did he write?"

"Poems."

"Such as?"

"Erm… 'O Time! Suspend thy flight!…'"

"And then how does it go?"

"Then, erm…"

"'And you, propitious hours / Suspend your course,'" the Sun whispers.

Great. The Sun can recite French poetry from memory. It's beginning to get a little hot, standing in his light.

Hakima: "How do you know that, Kader?"

"I learnt it."

"At school?"

"No. I was bored last year in my bedroom. I had a book, *The 100 Most Beautiful French Poems*."

"Did you learn any others?"

"All of them."

"All?"

"I was really *really* bored."

The Sun, when he is bored, learns poems by heart. Even though I hate all romantic things and cheesy stuff like that, it's obviously a good effort that it would be nice to encourage. So I encourage him, in a ridiculously high-pitched voice. "Oh, Kader, you'll have to recite poems to us on the way."

"Bah, you know, most of them are rubbish."

We cycle off, and my heart is a little bit like one of those moronic moths that knock themselves out on garden lamps. Kader's a light inside a globe, and me, I'm fluttering around it, going *bump, bump, bump*, against the glassy shell.

In the afternoon, pedalling gets harder because of the heat. We've trained mornings and evenings, but we've never done so many miles under the 2 to 6 p.m. sun, a great big macho sun that tramples us underfoot. Nothing like the canary-yellow sunshine that licks your face like a friendly Labrador when you leave home at six in the morning; nothing like the anaemic sun of summer evenings, weary and sweet, ready to brush its teeth and go to bed.

Right now, on the sinuous little roads snaking between vineyards—so many vineyards, blimey—there's not a shadow of a shadow, and right now, as we tow that trailer, which is only lighter by barely two dozen sausages, as I watch the Sun's arms going—*up and down and up and down*—and feel rivulets of sweat sliding down my spine, accumulating at the top of my shorts, right where a corkscrew of a tail would bud if I were a little piggy—right now, we get it: this trip is going to be hard.

It's not even that hot—20, 22 degrees...

"I've got a stitch," Astrid declares.

"Astrid, don't even joke about it. It's much too soon for that."

"It's not my fault if I've got a stitch," she retorts weakly.

"Breathe. Stitches happen when your muscles are deprived of oxygen and produce too much lactic acid. Just breathe and it'll be fine."

"Oh, thank you so much for telling me that, Mireille, because I'd been holding my breath for two hours just to see how long I can last."

The Sun: "Calm down, everyone. Let's slow down, if you like. No need to rush. We've got a shortish journey, today."

"It feels exactly like I'm being stabbed," Astrid moans.

Me: "I doubt it, but if you like we could stop and compare."

"Very funny."

"Stop talking!" the Sun shouts. "It messes with your breathing. That's why you get stitches."

The Sun is right, of course: I've barely said three sentences and I've got a stitch. Bloody lactic acid! It feels exactly like... I'm being stabbed.

We keep pedalling, sulking.

"Ouchy-ouch."

"Shush, Astrid."

That said, I'm secretly hoping she might beg us to stop so I can have a legitimate excuse to rest, since that bloody lactic acid is starting to nibble its way up under my ribcage.

"Ouch!"

"For God's sake, shut up, Astrid! What if you were a caveman being chased by a cyber-toothed tiger? Would you be hopping around going 'Ouch, ow, ouch, I've got a stitch'?"

"*Sabre*-toothed," says Hakima.

"Shall we stop?" says the Sun.

"No way. We keep going."

"Mireille..."

"OH! LOOK!" Hakima exclaims. "The Rock of Solutré!"

We look.

"It's amazing!" Hakima goes, jumping up and down with happiness. "I've always wanted to see it!"

"How do you know about it?"

"We learnt about it in Year 5."

Ah yes: she was in Year 5 only a few years ago. Thinking of tiny little Year 5 Hakima makes me go all mushy like a sweet little grandma. "Why have you always wanted to see it?"

"Just look at it! Look!"

We look, still pedalling along the road.

The Rock of Solutré is what the big rock in *The Lion King* would look like if it had landed at the heart of Burgundy, between the yellow and purple vineyards streaked with white paths. It's huge, like a block of earth pushed up by the elbow of a buried giant in his sleep. It's white, this afternoon, under the sun; clusters of little bushes make it look like a scabby knee. It hovers above the valley like the prow of a gigantic ship, which any second now will emerge from the earth, sail across the fields and take off, crumbling a little, sweeping the ground with a trail of ivy, climbing all the way to the bobble-like clouds above our heads...

"Oww-ouch," Astrid growls.

I oww-ouch silently too, with similar energy. Just bugger off, lactic acid!

"We learnt about it in Year 5, the Rock of Solutré," Hakima repeats. "You know the thing about the horses? The thing about the horses is that prehistoric men used to chase wild horses all the way to the top of the rock, so they were like, running, running, running, with lances and guns and everything, and the horses were so scared they were like, galloping, galloping, galloping, cos they were so scared, so they were galloping to the top of the rock, and the men would push them, and the horses would fall down, and tumble to the bottom, *crash!* and they'd burst into bits. So the men would eat them because they were dead."

"Very good, Hakima," says the Sun, "except they didn't have guns at the time."

Astrid and I stare at the rock, and maybe it's the heat, or the lactic acid, but it seems to me that I can see it all:

125

brown horses, galloping like mad, neighing with anger and fear, chased by scruffy cavemen—the horses losing their footing and hoofing the air, opening wide, white eyes, and—*crash!*—as Hakima says—shattering into pieces at the bottom...

"Like Mufasa," Hakima sighs respectfully.

"That was very clever, when you think about it," Astrid remarks. "Nice geostrategy."

"*Nice geostrategy?*"

She nods. "Yeah, that's exactly the kind of thing you need to think about. For instance, in *Survival Now III*, when you're stuck on the desert island, in order get off it you've got to optimize the island's resources, flora and fauna, and the solution's not obvious, oh no, believe me, you've got to find it out by your—"

"Astrid?"

"Hmm?"

"Your stitch has gone, then?"

"Oh! Yes, apparently."

"Mine too. Hakima, please keep some stories ready for the next lactic-acid attack."

15

We get to Cluny around six, and set up shop next to a huge stone building called Cluny Abbey (according to a board). But no sooner have we opened the trailer than...

"Hey! Look! It's the piglettes!"

...a tall Mediterranean girl rushes up to us. She's got fire-black, smoke-frizzy hair, and she's wearing the kind of dress you'd see at the Oscars—the blood-red, full-length glimmer of a million vermilion sequins. Behind her are a tall, brown-haired man and a tall blonde girl, both wearing a kind of military uniform, complete with gold braids and army caps.

These three elongated types flash us some remarkably flawless smiles.

"Great, they're right on time!" the dark-haired woman comments, consulting the brown-haired man's wristwatch.

"You'd like a sausage?" the Sun asks, a little stunned.

"Oh! I guess, if it makes you happy," says the dark-haired woman. "Gab? Blondie? Sausage? I haven't got any money, though."

Gab fishes a few coins from a pocket of his uniform. He buys a thyme sausage with onion sauce for Blondie, a plain sausage with apple sauce for himself, and a vegetarian sausage with mustard sauce for the tall dark-haired one, who "hates sweet-and-savoury stuff".

We watch the handsome trio eating our sausages. Even the Sun looks a little fascinated by the spectacle.

After some time, I dare to ask, "Sorry, Mr and Mrs Soldier and Mrs Princess Jasmine from *Aladdin*, would you mind telling us why you're dressed like that?"

Blondie bursts out laughing. "We're not soldiers, we're students here. Well, my brother Gab and I are. This is our university's official uniform. Bit military, I know, but I don't generally go waddling through mud with a gun if I can avoid it. Still, we have to wear it: it's the university's summer ball, tonight. And this is Coline, my brother's girlfriend."

We might have guessed, since Coline/Jasmine and Gab, their sausages barely swallowed, have been repeatedly clashing their lips together, as loudly and unsubtly as a pair of cymbals.

"They're super in love," Blondie explains.

"Looks like it," I admit. "What was that about a ball?"

"You'll soon see," Coline says slurpingly, having detached her mouth from Gab's with a bizarre sucking noise. "You're coming too."

"Who, us?" asks Hakima. "No, we can't, because after this service we've still got some cycling to do. We have to get to Taizé, don't we, Mireille? Taizé's where we're sleeping this eve—"

"No way!" Blondie interrupts her. "Listen, it'd be so fun: we're smuggling you into the summer ball!"

"You're *what*?!"

The Sun, in his wheelchair, has grown noticeably tense. With a sweep of the hand, Gab points out the huge abbey, behind which the sun is about to dive.

"That monastery, dear piglettes, isn't just a typical example of... erm..."

"Of Perpendicular Gothic architecture!" his sister fills in.

"Nonsense," snorts Coline, "it's totally Romanesque."

"Anyway," says Gab, "that monastery isn't just a perpendicularly romantic example of some architecture from some time in history. No, dear friends: it is also a prestigious school of engineering, where my sister and I are currently studying. That noble and ancient institute—"

"...gives a sumptuous ball every summer," Blondie says, picking up the thread. "The Summer Ball."

"Boring name, great ball," yawns Coline.

"And this year, it's tonight! You're right on time to get in."

"It's really nice of you to ask," says Astrid, "but we're not going to any balls, we're just selling sausages and cycling. And we have to get up early tomorrow, because we've got a lot of cycling and selling sausages to do."

"Astrid's right," I say.

"Oh, Astrid," Coline groans, "enjoy life a bit. It's a once-in-a-lifetime opportunity! This isn't a disco at the local youth club, my friends. It's one of the most coveted parties in Europe!"

Me: "If that's so, I can't see how we'd get in wearing shorts and sweaty T-shirts."

"No worries," Gab replies. "We've got it sorted."

Coline squeezes the lacy collars of three shiny dresses out of a plastic bag. Blondie turns to the Sun and smiles. "Sorry, we didn't think of bringing *you* clothes—you've got to admit, they're mostly talking about those three in the papers. But don't worry, we'll find you a suit somewhere. Gab, be a dear and lend a suit to... to..."

"Kader," the Sun whispers, and stares at Blondie as if he finds her attractive or something, which kind of gets on my nerves, because, well, apart from the fact that she's lithe, blonde, tall, with teeth as straight as piano keys and delicately turned ankles, she doesn't look *that* extraordinary.

"Sure," says Gab. "You must be about my height."

"Trousers might be a bit long," the Sun retorts. "Come on, guys. Seriously, why do you want to get us in there? You want to make fun of the girls? I'm meant to be looking after them."

"Oh, Kader!" pipes Blondie. "Kader darling, it's like you've never been a student."

"I haven't," says the Sun.

That shuts them up for a few seconds, but then Blondie starts again. "All right, but you've been a soldier, right? You probably know more than us about jokes and pranks. You've never made an apple-pie bed?"

"Sure, I have."

"You've never propped a bucketful of water on top of a door?"

130

"Yeah."

"You've never smuggled girls into the barracks?"

"Erm, no."

(*Quite right!*)

"OK, but you get what I mean. In this university, pranks are our religion. Well, pranks and gambling."

"And alcohol!" Gab chimes in.

"Alcohol?!" (A horrified echo from Hakima.)

"Gab, stop freaking them out," says Coline. "Anyway—this morning, a bunch of our friends read about you in the papers, and saw that you were stopping in Cluny this evening. They challenged us to smuggle you all into the ball tonight. If we do it, they're buying us a case of champagne."

"Each," Blondie specifies.

"No, no, no!" Hakima shrieks. "Mum and Dad don't want me to go to rave parties. Do they, Kader?"

"Course they don't," the Sun mutters unconvincingly. "It's out of the question."

"And what would *we* get out of it, anyway?" I ask. "We don't like champagne."

"I don't mind champagne," Astrid whispers.

"What would *you* get out of it?" Gab laughs. "She's asking what they'd get out of it? Oh please, Mireille—that's your name, isn't it?—Mireille, darling, come on..."

He slings an arm round my shoulders.

"You'll have the time of your *life*!"

———

131

A few minutes later, Coline has transformed the trailer into a changing room. Our fiery fairy godmother twirls in a circle, brandishing dresses, brushes, combs, needles, shawls and jewellery.

Hakima goes in first, looking like she's about to have her wisdom teeth extracted without anaesthetic. Waiting for the metamorphosis to occur, Gab and Blondie take Astrid and me to the secret medieval passageway we'll have to go down later.

"It's right by that plastic garden chair," says Gab. "Here's the key. The passage leads to the library. Everyone knows about it, so it'll be guarded by some nerds who volunteered as security officers. We'll distract them with firecrackers. As soon as you hear the bangs, get out of the passage, run to the red curtains and wait for us. We'll pick you up asap."

Coline pops her head out of the trailer and calls Astrid, who scuttles off. Me: "But once we're inside, they'll spot us straightaway! We're much younger than everyone else."

"No one'll pay any attention. We'll just avoid the wardens. Don't do anything too noticeable, and it will be fine."

Coline reappears. It's my turn.

The trailer's completely different now: the mini fridge has been turned into a make-up console, myriad pins are scattered on the floor. My dress awaits, duck-egg blue, draped across pots of sauce.

"Slip it on!"

"It's too long."

"No problem, we'll take it up. With safety pins, of course—no time to sew. But it'll do."

"How about my shoes?"

"Keep your trainers on—they'll be hidden by the dress. And just in case you've got to run..."

She winks at me and starts doing my hair, which is notoriously uninteresting: grey-squirrel-coloured, flat, dry. She manages to pull it up into a ball, ripping off half my scalp in the process, and punches dozens of glittery hairpins through it.

She then slathers my face in make-up and even spends some time painting my eyebrows, an art whose existence I had never suspected before.

"All done! Go and find your friends."

"Where are they?"

"In the museum toilets. You won't recognize them."

The decidedly multifunctional Cluny Abbey, which is also a university, is indeed also a museum, though that part's closed tonight, for ball-related reasons. The museum shop, however, is open, and so are the toilets near it. I slip into the building. A couple of tourists in shorts stare at me with interest. A father tells his kid, "You see, that's one of the young ladies who are going to the ball this evening."

"Come on, Gaëtan, it can't be," whispers his wife. "She's much too young to be studying here."

"Maybe she's the girlfriend of one of the students here," Gaëtan hypothesizes.

The girlfriend of a student. That good man considers it plausible that I might be the girlfriend of a student! With a thumping heart and reddened cheeks, I seek shelter in the toilets, where Hakima and Astrid, planted in front of a floor-to-ceiling mirror, are gazing at themselves with no small degree of surprise.

"Oh, it's..." I begin—but somehow, I cannot speak.

Who are they?

In the huge glistening mirror, three strangers—three young ladies—are looking at us. Who *are* they?

A voluptuous, curvaceous blonde, her egg-yolk-coloured, strapless dress ideally matched to her rosy complexion. Astrid? Astrid, is that really you?

And this perky little dark-haired girl, whose purple, off-the-shoulder velvet number sways like an anemone every time she moves around—Hakima? Hakima, is that you?

And that proud-looking young woman, her hair pulled back by diamond pins, her azure dress, pleated like a toga, falling over her endless legs and describing her pretty waist... is that... could that be... *me?*

...

JUST KIDDING!

We look exactly like what we are: three little piglettes, dressed up in synthetic ball dresses and painted like stolen cars. Astrid and I look like plumper versions of Cinderella's sisters Anastasia and Drizella in the Disney cartoon. Hakima has all the allure of a dried prune wrapped in bacon.

We're silent for a while, and then...

...and then we can't hold it any more—we burst out laughing; we double over with laughter—a laughter that

134

rises from the depths of our podgy bellies, that shakes our jewellery, our hair and our dresses—that forces us to lean against the taps—a laughter that makes us want to pee, a gigantic laughter of freedom and ecstasy, brand new, magnificent—as big and as spectacular as the ball that opens its doors to us, and soon swallows us up.

Blondie, Coline and Gab weren't lying: the ball is bewilderingly brilliant.

Huddled together like three lost ducklings, we hop from room to room, hypnotized. Each room, Gab explains, has been decorated by one of the year groups.

"That one's by those who matriculated last year."

"Who did *what*?" whispers Hakima, turning bright red.

"Nothing rude, my love, it just means enrolled."

"So it's the second years' room," explains Astrid. "It's as if your year entirely redecorated a room in our school, Hakima."

"Oh, right. Well, we'd start with taking down all the posters about abortion, drugs and bullying, because they're depressing," Hakima thinks out loud.

"Hey, look! This is Gab's year's room!" Coline says proudly, dragging us to a kind of frozen, apocalyptic wasteland.

"The theme was *Titanic*," Gab explains.

Stalactites—some real, some plastic—hang from the ceiling, dripping cold water onto our heads. In lieu of a bar, an ice wall, with carved-out nests for bottles. Loudspeakers are playing a mixture of sea noises and shrieks of terror, provoking laughter from the revellers. Some of them are trying on life jackets. A bunch of violinists are playing very sad music, and sometimes a foghorn may be heard.

"It's in very good taste!" I observe.

"Always!" Gab laughs.

We sit down in a lifeboat with a small round table in the middle.

"I had to hammer that bloody thing in," Gab says. "It was tricky as hell. I even swallowed a nail."

"You swallowed a nail?!" Hakima cries. "But you're going to die!"

"Oh, no, I don't think so," says Gab. "I ate a whole pack of cotton wool afterwards, it should be fine."

Hakima whispers to us, "Now he's got *twice* the amount of iron you're supposed to have in your body!"

Coline comes back with two Bellinis, one for her and one for Gab, and three alcohol-free cocktails for the other piglettes and me. Hakima sips hers, looking very much like she's suspecting it might secretly contain alcohol. She grumbles, "Where's Kader, anyway?"

Apparently, no need to worry: the Sun makes his entrance in a dashing suit, pushed merrily by Blondie, who got him into the ball by saying loudly, "He's my new boyfriend, I know he hasn't got a ticket, but come on, he's disabled! You just have to let him in!"

He whistles when he sees us. "Gorgeous! You look like Hollywood actresses. Mireille, that hairstyle really suits you."

"Oh! Pff! Hmmph!" I reply, and go on emitting another dozen equally weird noises. Said hairstyle has a major flaw, that of revealing my ears, which must be visibly Merlot-coloured right about now.

The Sun declines the Bellini offered by Blondie, and calmly drinks a Coke while she downs a cocktail in a few minutes.

"Where did you change clothes, Kader?" Hakima asks.

"Oh, just over there, in a room."

"In Blondie's room?"

He drinks his glass instead of replying, masking a small smile I wish I could X-ray.

"Unbelievable, this ball," he murmurs, half-amused, half-reproachful. "Does it happen every year?"

"Every year! We need to celebrate, you see, after all the work we've done!"

The Sun nods, but I know what he's thinking; he's thinking that in the army, you don't celebrate the end of the year with pretty balls when you've lost yet another, I don't know, fifty, sixty soldiers in Problemistan, not to mention the Sun's bottom half. He's also thinking about Barack Obamette, who promised, crossed her heart and hoped to die, that the troops would be pulled out this year, but eventually she just couldn't, you see, because the Americans wouldn't be pleased, and it's all very complicated.

I wonder if Klaus Von Strudel is annoyed that his wife's sending all those men to die in Problemistan so as not to displease the Americans?

Hey, it's been a while since I've thought about Klaus.

We walk around, changing rooms and atmospheres. A jungle here, a beach there, and in corridor after corridor, room after room, we help ourselves generously to paella, oysters, cheeses, cakes—and alcohol, too. I try sangria, just to see what it's like, in the flamenco room; and caipirinha, just to see what it's like, in the salsa room... We keep walking, brushing past crinoline dresses (who still wears crinoline dresses?), tail coats (who still wears tails?) and school uniforms.

Suddenly, Blondie spots a richly decorated, Versailles-style room, where an elegant waltz is playing, and...

"Kader, you're dancing with me!"

"Course not."

"It wasn't a question..."

Well, apparently he can dance. With Blondie, he can dance. That wheelchair isn't just good for playing Paralympic basketball, it seems—you can also kind of waltz around. As long as there's a tall blonde to swirl around, like a satellite around one's solar chariot...

"Astrid, Mireille... he's dancing. He's dancing!" Hakima murmurs. "I must tell Jamal. And Mum. And Dad. And cousin Sofia and Auntie Nour..."

Me: "Come on, let's get out of here."

"Why?"

"I really want to see that room over there. It looks awesome!"

That room over there that looks awesome, and which I've picked entirely at random, turns out to be the karaoke room, where a chubby man is currently attempting to sing some Avril Lavigne. We sit down and clap loudly—me especially, because the two cocktails are starting to make their way into my bloodstream...

"Let's all give Jean-François a big round of applause!" the karaoke's emcee shouts.

Me (I think): "Woohoo! Jean-François, you're the best!" *[whistle]*

"Mireille, are you drunk?"

"Me? Drunk? Lies! Jean-François, another one! Encore! Encore!"

Jean-François looks a teensy bit taken aback to be begged for more songs by Cinderella's stepsister, but he flashes me a goofy smile. Uh-oh, looks like we've been spotted.

"Hey, we've got a lovely trio over there!" the emcee yells. "Aren't you going to sing us a little something? How about the Spice Girls?"

"NO WAY, MATE!" I shout back (at least I think it's me). "I SING ALMOST AS BADLY AS JEAN-FRANÇOIS!"

"And I don't know any songs," Hakima worries.

"How about you, in the middle? Want to sing us something?"

It takes Astrid two and a half centuries to realize he's talking to her. "Who, me?"

"YES, YOU!" everyone else shouts (including me, I believe).

"Well, I dunno," says Astrid. "Have you got any Indo-chine songs?"

"She's asking if we've got any Indochine songs!" the emcee laughs. "Of course we've got Indochine songs, my love! Which one do you want?"

"Well, I..." Astrid stammers. "Well... any of them..."

"Then here we go!" the emcee yells. "Hop on stage, young lady!"

"COME ON, ASTRID!!!" screams someone, who happens to be me. "YOU'RE GONNA SMASH IT!!!"

She gets to the stage, shaking like she's riding her own personal earthquake, huge rings of sweat blossoming under her armpits.

"AS-TRID! AS-TRID!" the crowd chants.

She's onstage!

Terrified, petrified.

Dumbstruck.

And then we hear the first few chords...

...and she picks up the mic.

"The screen's over there," the emcee says. "So you can see the lyrics."

But Astrid answers, contemptuously:

"I don't need the lyrics."

The first riff—synthetic, electrifying. Having never listened to Indochine, or indeed to any synthetic or electrifying music, I have no idea what to expect. But she's going to open her mouth, I can tell—she's going to sing, in five, four, three, two...

"Lost-his-path in the valley of hell / Our hero's name is—Bob Morane!..."

I turn to Hakima, who's as wide-eyed as me. The other

140

members of the audience are also doing pretty convincing impressions of Japanese koi carp. While I'm wondering what this absurd music is about, people around me laugh, clap, and say "Who *is* that girl? How weird is it that a girl her age is singing Indochine? How weird is it she's singing Indochine so bloody well? She's a natural, that one, a natural!"

A natural: Astrid onstage, stealing the show from that singer whose picture is pinned everywhere on her bedroom walls, in her diary, on her T-shirts...

"Bob Morane isn't scared of lions... / When adventure awaits, he cuts to the chase... oh yes!"

(Her voice goes up eight octaves and then down again.)

The crowd is hysterical.

The night is historical.

The song stops much too early. I want more! We all do!

"Ladies and gentlemen, Astrid!"

"ASTRIIIIIIIIIIIIIIIIIIIIIIIIIID!" scream the floor-length-gowned ladies and the tuxedoed gentleman.

"Wait a minute!" someone says. "SHE'S ONE OF THE PIGLETTES!"

An abrupt silence, and some perplexed chuckles. A very tipsy man hauls himself up onstage, falls on his face, pulls himself up using Astrid's dress. "Frédo! Coco!" he shouts to two of his friends in the audience. *"They did it!* Blondie and Gab! They smuggled in the Three Little Piglettes!"

The emcee, slightly overwhelmed by the situation, shakes his head awkwardly. "What piglets?"

"The other two are over there, at the back! Come onstage, girls! Come on! Don't be shy! Blimey, guys—we'll have to get Gab and Blondie those cases of champagne!"

There's no way I'm going up on stage. *No way*, I'm telling you: no, no, I'm not that kind of person. Yet I appear to be standing up—proudly—and soon I begin to walk mechanically forward, dragging Hakima with me. Shortly thereafter, I'm hanging from Astrid's neck, waving to the crowd and screaming, "WHAT D'YOU SAY??? WHO'S THE BEST??? THAT'S RIGHT: THE THREE LITTLE PIGLETTES!"

Flash, flash, flash. I can guess what those emperor penguins and pretty ladies are typing on their phones, in the light-blue and navy squares of Twitter and Facebook accounts: *#3littlepiglettes at the Cluny Campus Summer Ball!*

Uh-oh, looks like security's spotted us, too...

"Thank you again! *Grazie mille! Muchas gracias!*"

Coline, in fits of laughter: "You're welcome! Now get out of here, quick!"

"But the dr-dresses! They're yours!"

"Doesn't matter, off with you!"

"Won't you be in tr-trouble because of us?"

"Run, Mireille! Come on, off you go already!"

Under the huge moon, tripping over our ball dresses, we clamber onto our bikes and rush off, dragging our trailer, following the Sun—whose pace is a little less energetic than usual, as if he's already missing the ball he danced so well at...

142

(At the gate of the abbey, meanwhile, security guards have formed a reception committee for the giggling Gab, Blondie and Coline.)

The bell tower rings twelve times...

"Disaster! The coach is gonna turn back into a pumpkin! Watch out!... One! Two!..."

"Mireille..."

"To Taizé and beyooooond!"

"Mireille?"

"Yeah?"

"Did you have a bit too much to drink?"

"Enough to fuel myself all the way to Taizé! Come on, hurry up! We need to get there before night-time!"

"It *is* night-time."

"Well, then, before, erm, three in the morning."

"She's sozzled," Astrid confirms. "Mireille, I suggest we stop and set up camp."

"NO! We said we were going to Taizé! That's the plan! We can't be late, ooooh no!"

"Stop shouting. We'll get arrested for disturbing the peace."

"What does the Sun think? Hey! The Sun! I'm talking to you! Are we going to Taizé or what?"

The Sun, of course, doesn't realize I'm talking to him; everyone thinks I'm attempting to disturb the peace of the whole solar system. Still wearing Gab's costume, he's propelling himself a few yards in front of us, on the deserted road.

"Kader!" Hakima begs. "Tell Mireille we're tired and we have to stop."

"Mireille," the Sun laughs, "we're tired and we have to stop."

So we stop, for we must obey that divine command. Sunset time.

No campsite in sight. We set up camp on a strip of soft grass alongside a vineyard. We park the trailer, unfold the tents...

"Look! If I spread it like that, it's like I have wings!"

"You're smashed, Mireille."

"I belieeeeeve I can flyyyy!"

"Mireille?"

"Yes, Astrid darling, object of my unending adoration? Ooooh, do you want to sing us another song? Please, another song—a little lullaby."

"No. Go to bed."

"OK. You share your tent with Hakima and I'll share mine with the Sun. I mean, with Kader."

"No, Hakima's sleeping in Kader's tent. They're siblings, it's only right."

"It's entirely *wrong*, you mean! Oh, shucks! I should have called dibs!"

I can't quite remember slithering into my sleeping bag, but I must have managed it, since I wake up the next morning in the distinctive and peculiarly damp atmosphere of a tent, the karaoke heroine snoring tunefully at my side.

THE THREE LITTLE PIGLETTES DO KARA-*OINK*-E AT THE CLUNY CAMPUS BALL!

The "Three Little Piglettes", as they are now known, were reportedly spotted at the prestigious Summer Ball at Cluny Abbey yesterday evening.

According to witnesses, the three teenagers, wearing ball gowns, sang karaoke and drank alcohol. The students' committee is investigating the matter. In a telephone conversation this morning, Mireille Laplanche denied being there, and insists that the "Three Little Piglettes" are currently on their way to Montceau-les-Mines after a night camping near Cluny.

H.L.

Piglettes on the Net: click for a slideshow of pictures taken by Cluny Ball guests.

("Mireille, did you illegally gatecrash the Cluny Campus Ball?"

"Oh, Mummy! Always those big bad words."

"Did you drink alcohol?"

"An infinitesimal amount!"

"Where's my manuscript gone?"

"What manuscript, venerated mother?"

"The one that was in my desk drawer. *Being and Bewilderment.*"

"Has it vanished? How bewildering. Must be Philippe Dumont trying to read it. Argh, sorry, Mummy, time to go, I'm running out of battery, and we need to get a move on, we're expected in Montceau-les-Mines and we're just going into a tunn...")

16

I'm not even slightly hungover; not even the merest mini-migraine. Just goes to show it's all lies and scare-mongering, what they say about alcohol.

I wake up before everyone else. All crinkly in my ball dress, a thousand hairpins digging into my scalp, I sit outside the tent on a flat stone, staring at the grapevines with their gnarls of frogspawn-like grapes. At this time of the year, they're cheek-puckeringly sour.

You never sleep well in a tent; you're either too cold or too hot, and you hold your pee in for hours so your bladder swells against the hard floor and you wake up with a stomach ache. But I feel calm, rested. It's barely six in the morning, so I've had barely six hours' sleep.

I change quickly behind a tree, wash off some of my make-up with water from a bottle we'd filled in Mâcon, and unlock my bike to go on a breakfast hunt. Between the vineyards shimmer the mirage-like image of a picturesque farmhouse, in front of which two flea-sized dogs are hopping and playing. Memories of picture books from my childhood conjure up in my mind a grumpy, mustachioed farmer, who's holding a big German shepherd by its collar when it barks as I draw near. The farmer's wife, busy but tender-hearted, sells us six eggs in a basket lined with feathers and chicken droppings, a little pot of milk, a loaf of bread—and maybe she'll tell us a little story about her life too...

"What do you want?" the grumpy farmer asks as I draw near. (He is much younger than in the picture books from my childhood, and has neither a dog nor a moustache.)

"Good morning, sir. I'm camping over there with some friends, and I'd like to buy eggs, perhaps, or bread, or butter, or milk..."

The grumpy farmer scratches his head. His busy but tender-hearted wife turns up (also young, and wearing Converse). I reiterate my request.

"OK, if you want..." she says. "Well, we don't have any eggs, I don't think, but... hang on, I'll be back in a minute."

She comes back two minutes later with a bag of sliced supermarket bread, a small jar of Nutella and a bottle of pasteurized milk.

"It's all I could find in our cupboard."

Right, so they aren't exactly farmers—they sell huge farming machines from a hanger. I decide to keep that detail quiet as I watch Astrid, Hakima and the Sun enthusiastically bite into the grumpy-farmer-and-busy-but-tender-hearted-wife-sourced Nutella sandwiches.

"Are we still going to Montceau-les-Mines for lunch?" asks Astrid, post-food.

"Yes. It's only three hours from here, at a stretch. We'll need to find a place where we can charge the mini fridge—the battery must be almost flat. It'd be good if we could avoid infecting the whole region with cholera."

"Mireille, were you really drunk last night, or just pretending?"

"Just pretending, of course, Hakima."

"And you, Kader, were you really in love with Blondie, or just pretending?"

"You don't fall in love in just one evening."

"You were doing a good impression of it."

And she wolfs down another sandwich. The Sun, the shadow of a smile on his lips, hauls himself into his wheelchair and slips on his gloves. Even with their protection, though, his palms are blistered, bleeding in some places and scabbed in others.

"We could do with a coffee machine in that trailer."

"Don't tell me you need any more energy, Kader!" Astrid chuckles. "Seeing how much you danced last night... Show me? Nope, doesn't look like you're wasting away..."

She *squeezes his biceps.*

I repeat: *Astrid squeezes the Sun's biceps.*

Just for fun.

As we get back onto our bikes, I ask: "Astrid, are you a lesbian?"

"No. Well... I don't think so. Why?"

"You just squeezed Kader's biceps."

"Yeah, as a joke. So what?"

"So what? So you didn't spontaneously dissolve into a pool of goo! You didn't instantaneously jump from one state of matter to the next!"

"Er, no."

"Well, QED, and *cogito ergo sum*."

"Which means?"

"You are a lesbian."

As she ponders the validity of my logic, we set off ("Ready? One, two, three...") behind the Sun, who leads us on our way.

The road between the fields is freshly tarmacked and beautifully smooth. Back in the trailer, our dresses, pretty mementoes of yesterday's party, are jostling for space with our sausages. Because I'm an idiot, I stuffed all my hairpins into my shorts pockets, and now they're pecking at my thighs every time I push down on the pedals. But who cares? There's a light breeze, the blue sky is freckled with clouds and the way ahead is flat—for now. We decided to skirt around the mountains of the Morvan, knowing we'd have a tough time of it on that terrain; so, from tomorrow, we'll be following the banks of the River Loire. Fret not, I have no idea where all those places are either—we're trusting our faithful GPS.

Cars overtake us once in a while, as well as tractors and the occasional combine harvester. They drive past us slowly, no stress. It suddenly dawns on me that cycling into Paris won't be quite as relaxing. But we'll cross that bridge when we come to it.

Suddenly, as we round a corner, a thousand birds dart out of a bush, and the flock flies up, then down, then up again, before getting sucked in by another bush...

It's bliss. Perfect bliss.

Until Hakima moans, "I'm... I'm really sorry, girls, but I've got a really, really, really bad stomach ache."

Astrid throws me a worried glance, probably concerned I might behead little Hakima with one mighty blow of my bike pump. In order to ascertain whether that will be necessary, however, I first ask, "How big are we talking?"

"Like yesterday, but worse."

"You had a bellyache yesterday? Why didn't you say anything?"

"I didn't want to be a bother..."

"Well, that's silly, we could have got you some medicine in Cluny. Is it like diarrhoea pain?"

Out of the corner of my eye, I can see her face flaming up. "A bit, but it's lower down... I don't know, it's so weird. I've never had it before."

And she carries on moaning. The Sun turns his head towards us, seems to want to say something, and then doesn't. I tell Hakima, "It'd better not be gallstones, I'm warning you! We're in the middle of nowhere here. You get internal bleeding, we're dumping you into a ditch."

"Stop it, Mireille, you're not funny," Astrid frowns. "Hakima, shall we take a break?"

"Nnno... I don't want to make us late..." Hakima moans again.

That moan (the third one) breaks my little heart. I'm like that deep-down, really, a sensitive soul. "Of course we'll take a break. Don't worry. The GPS says there's a campsite not too far away, near a lake. We'll just go slightly off-route, set up shop there, charge the fridge batteries, sell our sausages to the campers, and then cycle off again when you're feeling better—OK?"

"But Montceau-les-Mines..."

"We won't go to Montceau-les-Mines. We'll cut straight to the next stop. The lady in the GPS will recalculate our journey; she does that very well. All right?"

Hakima breathes an *all right* through nostrils clogged with tears and snot. I suddenly remember she only started high school last year and I feel like hugging her very tight. Well, not right now—we've still got a twenty-minute cycle to the campsite.

"Do you really think it's flintstones?" Hakima asks shyly.

"Gallstones. Course not. It must be a minor case of food poisoning. Don't worry, Hakima. We won't dump you in a ditch. It was just a funny joke of the highest order. Come on, we'll get there soon, and you won't have to sell any sausages."

As we're pedalling, the Sun turns to me, nods and mouths a *thank you*.

———

LAKE ROUSSET CAMPSITE ★★

The lake that looked tiny on the GPS screen turns out to be vast, fringed with trees, reeds and wandering families, with laughing, sun-baked children running all over the place playing tag. Fishermen's boats and clouds' reflections slide across the shiny surface of the water, which is as smooth and green as a shard from a wine bottle.

The owner of the campsite is chewing mauve bubble gum and wearing a Tweety and Sylvester T-shirt. Our first attempts to convince her to let us have a spot for just a few hours are met with a mighty sulk. But suddenly—amazingly—she recognizes us.

"You're the Piglettes!"

"Oh, do you read the *Bresse Courier* website?"

"No. They were talking about you on TV."

On TV? Which channel? The lady can't remember; she keeps flicking between them all. Maybe it was BFM TV. Or maybe i>Télé, or maybe France 3 but it could have been LCI, too, or perhaps... Anyway, it was this morning and there were pictures of us leaving Bourg-en-Bresse.

I look at my phone while Hakima goes to the loo. I've got seven missed calls: two from Hélène Lesnout, one from Mum, and four from unknown numbers.

Six voicemails:

HÉLÈNE LESNOUT: "Hi, Mireille. As you can tell, people are getting interested in your little adventure. I just wanted to, well, I guess, make sure that I still had exclusive access to you and the girls? Right—I'm happy to drive up to wherever you are, just let me know where that is. Is that OK? Anyway—call me back, all right?"

MUM: "Mireille! Where are you all? Listen—this is getting completely out of hand. Call me back at once. Don't talk to the press. Hakima and Kader's parents are very worried. I hope Hakima hasn't read the comments under that BFM TV Web article."

SHY VOICE: "Oh, hello, Miss Laplanche, this is Marc Gammoneau, I'm a journalist at BFM TV... I'd like to know if perhaps I could have a little chat with you when you get to Montceau-les-Mines this evening?... Call me back on..."

HIGH-PITCHED VOICE: "Hi, Miss Laplanche, my name's Antonia Rashers, I'm an editorial assistant for i>Télé... Listen, I was wondering if you'd be up for answering a few questions by phone, as soon as possible really—my number is..."

CONFIDENT VOICE: "Hi there, I'm Guillaume Schwein, a reporter for *Le Parisien*. I got your number from a colleague of mine. I'm planning to write an article on that little trip of yours, so please call me on..."

HÉLÈNE LESNOUT (again): "Mireille, it's Hélène. I have no idea where you are, but I'd like to talk to you, if that's OK, so I can keep updating your story. We'll probably switch to the print edition for tomorrow's article. I also just wanted to make sure none of my fellow journalists have been trying to—well—I just wanted to make sure that—well, anyway, call me, please."

I hang up. "Christ on a bike! I don't know what's been happening, but all of a sudden everyone's paying attention."

"Can't get any signal," Kader grumbles, fiddling with his phone. "I'm sorry, have you got Wi-Fi here?"

"Yes, just connect to 'lakerousset' and fill in the form with your credit-card details. It's five euros an hour for daytime visitors."

Kader flashes his most dazzling smile. "Listen, how about we do a deal—give us your private username and password for free, and we'll mention Lake Rousset Campsite to all the journalists who ask. And say good things, of course."

The woman, halfway through blowing a gigantic bubble, blushes violently, coughs, returns the deflated bubble to its rightful place in her mouth, and whispers, "Erm... OK, then—but don't give it to anyone else, all right? The password is, er—J-C can keep it up for 45 mins—all lower case, with digits for forty-five."

Astrid, curious: "Who's J-C?"

"My husband, Jean-Claude. But don't go thinking it's true! It's just that the broadband guy said we had to have letters and numbers."

The Sun hums a little tune, pretending to have entirely missed that conversation, and taps his screen. Meanwhile,

Hakima comes back, whispers something in Astrid's ear, and both of them scuttle off together. Blessed be St Astrid of unending devotion; I can't stand moaning and whining. Julius-Aurelian had better soldier bravely through his teething pains, or Mum and Philippe Dumont won't be getting any babysitting out of me.

While Astrid "Florence Nightingale" Blomvall and her patient are away, I lean nonchalantly over the Sun's shoulder to look at the news.

One search for the word "Piglettes" in Google News, and we start to understand the scale of what's been happening.

"Twelve articles already this morning," the Sun mutters. "Where did it all come from?"

We can't tell, but the articles all say roughly the same thing: three little piglettes and a disabled man are cycling from Bourg-en-Bresse to Paris, selling sausages on the road. And wait for it: rumour has it they gatecrashed the Cluny Campus Ball. Is that all? Not quite! "The odyssey of these three very young women seems to be catching the imagination of social-media users, from Facebook to Twitter, who are discussing the unusual convoy," *Libération* reports. Why? According to *Metro*, "This road trip, by three girls who look nothing like TV stars, is a quirky revenge story that appeals to the bullied teen in all of us." *Le Figaro* goes further: "In contemporary youth culture, where harassment and beauty vlogging have replaced social cohesion and intellectual ambition, the self-proclaimed 'Three Little Piglettes', whose ultimate aims remain unknown, look set to make a big impression."

Little by little we come to understand that an influential feminist blogger, the pseudonymous Simone Suffragette, sparked all of this earlier today, with a blog post shared by hundreds of her followers. She thinks we're "exemplary", "smart and slightly nutty", and ends her post with a glorious flourish: "Yet more evidence, in case we really needed it after Malala Yousafzai, that young girls can be full of initiative." She also slams Malo, "that macho, middle-class little boy, a pitiful heir of generations of chauvinist pigs who think their Y chromosome gives them the right to comment on, classify and rank the bodies and faces of all women who dare to enter their 'territory'".

"Blimey," the Sun murmurs, "we didn't see *that* coming..."

Indeed. I'm a happy shade of pink, and I can hear the blood pounding in my ears (although the Sun's left shoulder being in direct contact with my forearm may have something to do with that too). Still, nothing to get big-headed about, oh no, not me. I don't aspire to celebrity, you see; I want a quiet little life, maybe one or two Nobel Prizes, that's all.

Well, I suppose I wouldn't mind Klaus Von Strudel signing an official scroll of parchment admitting to, first, his shameful desertion of me in my embryonic state, and second, the fact that he has in no way contributed to my becoming Mireille Laplanche, the eminent twenty-first-century intellectual.

Maybe, when I get awarded the Nobel Prize in Literature, I'll even tearfully thank Philippe Dumont, just to piss off Klaus.

In a beautifully nonchalant tone, I say, "Yes, it's interesting, isn't it. Journalists! We all know what they're like. Anyway, let's find a plug for that fridge. Madame, if our two friends come back, could you tell us we've gone to our spot?"

"Yes, no problem. And what if any journalists come?"

"They don't know where we are. We're not supposed to be here."

The owner, a bit awkwardly: "Ah. But let's say, for instance, that I had... let's say I'd tweeted, for instance, something like..."

Rousset Campsite @roussetcampsite
The #3littlepiglettes are selling sausages at #lakerousset #campsite!!!

———

"Mireille, I need to talk to you."

"Just a minute, Astrid. I'm in the middle of a sale."

"Yes, but it's important and Hakima doesn't want her brother to hear us."

"What sauce would you like, sir?... Onion, great, no problem! Why, what's wrong with Hakima? Hey, you know what, people are loving your apple compote."

"Mireille, seriously, I've got to talk to you."

"Hang on—sorry, Madame, what was that?... Yes, it's vegetarian, so by definition it's kosher... Yeah, like falafels... Of course, in a separate pan! And we store them separately, too!"

"Mireille! Hakima's on her period!"

"She hadn't worked out that it'd come in the middle of the trip?"

"*For the first time*, you idiot..."

Hakima's sitting on a bench, looking as if she's been afflicted with some existential crisis, her hands around her belly. It's like she's just been told she'll never be allowed to drink hot chocolate again for the rest of her life.

"Hey, Hakima, big day! Congratulations!"

"Hmmmgnnhmm."

"Have you taken any ibuprofen?"

"Yes, Astrid gave me some."

"You got tampons?"

Whoops, wrong word: her black eyes widen, affording me a glimpse of a cerebral antechamber containing all the horror in the world: I see ferocious battles, with people skewering each other with bayonets, and spiky-tailed demons slamming heavy rocks onto the fingers of the damned.

"Well, either that or pads."

"Yeah, Astrid bought me some from the vending machine in the toilet."

I sit down next to her. "Why didn't you tell me you'd got your period?"

"Dunno. I was afraid you might be like, *Oh, for goodness' sake, she's so annoying, with all her problems.*"

I start laughing, but it turns into a weird tearful thing. "Goodness, am I that scary?"

She shakes her head, but doesn't seem 100 per cent sure.

"No... but I knew I would better tell Astrid."

"I *had* better tell Astrid. Or, I *would rather* tell Astrid. Or, at a stretch, I *would* be *better off* telling Astrid."

"Does it always hurt like that?"

"Grammar? Yes, it's very painful."

"No, periods."

"Periods? Always at the end of a sentence; semicolons, however, are a far more elegant punctuation sign; they can be used repeatedly; good sentences, in fact, should never end."

"Stop making fun at me!"

"Making fun *of* me, or laughing *at* me."

"*Stop it!* See, that's why you're scarier than Astrid."

"Maybe, but you're smiling now."

"Yeah, a bit..."

"Come on, let's go for a swim—erm, well, not you, I guess, but you can watch."

"Can I call my mum on your mobile phone to tell her? I don't want Kader to know—promise me you won't tell Kader."

"Cross my heart, hope to die. I won't say a thing."

———

(Ten minutes earlier:

"My sister's got her period, hasn't she?"

"How do you know?"

"When a girl says her belly's hurting, then she locks herself in the loo with an older girl for ages, and then all three girls start whispering to each other in conspiratorial tones..."

"I don't know, it could have been a very discreet abortion.")

17

We left around 2 p.m., after going for a swim in Lake Rousset. Well, Astrid and I went, while the Sun kept Hakima company. We waded into the green water, and happily splashed around with the other swimmers. We felt like sisters, all complexes forgotten.

OK, that's a lie. The truth is, we went for a swim very, very far from the campsite, so as not to offer to the eyes of passers-by the spectacle of our tubby pink bellies, our far-too-close-together thighs and our pear-shaped bums.

To be clear: it's not that I don't like my body! It's just that I hate it.

I looked at Astrid out of the corner of my eye and compared myself to her. I nodded appreciatively to see that she really is much fatter than I am. But her boobs, to be fair, stand up on their own, whereas mine are permanently napping.

Yeah, I know. But what can you do? You can't always be happy to be a pig. I'm fifteen and a half. At my age, girls don't look like that. Not to me, anyway. Most of them look like elongated aliens from a science-fiction film, defying the laws of gravity with their mysteriously slim ankles.

When we got out of the water, a bunch of boys our age shouted at us that we'd better dive straight back in, since it's the natural environment *for whales like you, for fucking huge sea elephants like you.*

Thankfully, they didn't recognize us or take any pictures: no #bikinipiglettes for us.

"When you think about it, though," Astrid whispered, "we must have burnt a lot of calories today."

"That's not why we're doing this!" I barked at the superficial Swede.

"Oh, I know, I know, we don't care about that. I was just saying."

"It's inner beauty that counts," I said, wagging my index finger under her nose, busy counting in my head how many calories we might have burnt.

Luckily, I'm rubbish at mental arithmetic.

We leave without bumping into any journalists. The Sun tells us there're already two Facebook fan pages for us, both of which are very concerned with where we might be, who we are and why we're doing all this. And, apparently, Montceau-les-Mines is preparing a welcome for us.

Me, through clenched teeth: "What's that motorbike doing? Why isn't it overtaking?"

Astrid, look quickly to the side: "Seems like he's waving."

Hakima: "Maybe it's the police?"

"Let's slow down. Kader! We're slowing down!"

We stop by the kerb, next to a wheat field. But under the helmet, it isn't a police officer. It's a journalist.

"Audrey!" the journalist bleats into his phone. "I've found them! Yes, yes, definitely them." He pockets the phone, and tries (in vain) to shake our hands. "Very nice to meet you all. Mathieu Cauchon, of *Ouest-France*..."

"Sorry," Kader says, "we're not doing any interviews."

"I'm not talking to you, I'm talking to the little ladies."

"What little ladies? Can you see any little ladies? I can't see any little ladies," I say, and the four of us lean down to examine the gravel in the hope of spotting what I imagine to be a swarm of tiny women in Victorian dresses.

"Miss Laplanche," says the journalist in a slightly perplexed tone, "you're the spokesperson for the group, aren't you? May I ask you a few questions? When do you think you'll get to Paris?"

"Never, if we keep getting stopped on the way by journalists. Come on, team—back in the saddle!"

We cycle off, but it doesn't deter Cauchon, who follows us on the left side of the road, pulling back only to let the occasional car through. So we endure an hour of pedalling in the afternoon heat with a journalist incessantly yelling questions at us. Why are you going to Paris? How do you feel about the media craze around you? Do you think it's right that the police aren't interfering? Are you trying to

164

lose weight by cycling such a long way, or would it only be a welcome side effect?

"Are you ever going to leave us alone?" I finally break down. "This isn't the Tour de France! We're just trying to get to our next stop."

"Which is?"

I sigh, and look at the GPS. "Gueugnon. Wait for us there? Honestly, you're making this afternoon's ride a bit trying. And you're going to give us all asthma attacks with that exhaust pipe."

"Can I wait for you there with a photographer?"

"With a whole TV crew, if it makes you happy. On the main square. We'll get there in two, two and a half hours."

"See you then!"

And *vroooooom!* The motorbike roars off.

Phew.

At last.

Ah, silence!... The quiet, dark-grey, sun-roasted ribbon of the road, swirling through the hollows between the hills...

"We're turning right at the next junction."

"Right? But that sign said to go left for Gueugnon!"

"Yeah, Hakima, I know. *Precisely.*"

A few hours later, Hakima's belly starts to ache again, and Astrid starts complaining about a shooting pain in her back, and even the Sun half-heartedly alludes to a sore hand (oh! Sun! How I would nurse those hands, bathe them in ointments and precious balms, if you let me—and if the very thought weren't enough to burn me from the inside!)...

...and out of nowhere, a fairy-tale castle appears in front of us.

We've left the trailer and the bikes at the bottom of the road.

"What *is* that thing?"

"The castle of Longuemort, according to the GPS."

"Of *Voldemort?*" Hakima quivers. "Oh, let's not stay, then."

The Sun laughs, and pulls his little sister, exhausted by pedalling and puberty, onto what's left of his lap.

Astrid has lost her tongue. She's staring at the castle. At the top, slender turrets and elegant balconies climb to the skies. At the bottom sits a sturdy, red medieval fortress. It looks mismatched, a bit like a young lady with a hairy man's feet.

"The castle of Longuemort isn't open to visitors."

Although we'd have been forgiven for thinking otherwise, these words were not bleated by a goat, but by a very old person (man or woman? Who knows?) pushing a wheelbarrow full of flowers.

"We don't care, we didn't want to visit it," says Astrid.

The old person looks offended. (I spot some earrings under tufts of grey hair—a woman, then, maybe?) "Shame. The gardens and the building are magnificent."

"You've just told us we can't visit it, and now you're saying it's a shame?"

"It's a shame to miss out on so much beauty."

Nice. The old probably-lady opens a wrought-iron gate, leading to the gardens. The view is indeed sumptuous: parrot-green lawns, trees swarming with birds, and behind it all bushes and flower beds all tightly cropped in the Frenchest of styles, set against the white walls of the castle.

Before closing the gate, the old lady eyes us up. "What are you doing here at this time, anyway?"

"We're cycling from Bourg-en-Bresse to Paris," I explain. "The Three Little Piglettes. You haven't heard of us?"

Oh, a sudden raising of an eyebrow. Of course she watches TV, like all old people.

"No idea why," I keep going, "but it fascinates journalists. And we're trying to avoid them. So we ended up here. We're going to look for a place to have dinner and then set off again. We weren't lurking, we were just looking at your castle because it's pretty, that's all."

The old lady frowns. "It's not *my* castle—I'm just the warden. Come on, you might as well have dinner at mine. The owners aren't here, anyway."

"Oh, that's kind of you, but we really weren't trying to wangle an invite."

"No, please do come." Her face lights up. "It'd be a pleasure."

So we follow her, through the little gate and into the gardens of the castle of Longuemort.

"Are you sure?" Hakima asks us weakly. "We shouldn't follow people we don't know..."

167

"You're right, she might be a Death Eater."

"Stop making fun at me, Mireille!"

We fall silent as we walk by the dizzyingly deep moat, which is carpeted with grass. The low afternoon light is crayoning the castle walls pure white, in contrast with the stark black arrow slits at its top. A mosaic of perfectly manicured lawns, neat flower beds and sculpted bushes, the garden resonates with the buzzing of bees, which fly back and forth, bumping into roses and sipping nectar mid-flight from tiny, white, trumpet-shaped flowers whose name I don't know.

"Are there really people living here?" Kader asks.

"Not often. The family comes and goes. Most of the time, the only people here are the ones who work here and give guided tours."

The old lady's called Adrienne, and, she tells us as if it weren't out of the ordinary, she's ninety-five. She's almost always lived here, though she wasn't born here... (She gets her key out to open the door to her tiny house, near the castle.) Tonight, she's celebrating the birth, in Tokyo, of her first great-grand-niece. Her grand-nephew married a Japanese woman (something that Adrienne seems to find quite strange, but then again "they'd always been his type".) So the little girl will "no doubt have slanted eyes", but it "doesn't matter too much", she guesses, because "these days people come in lots of different colours". Her name is Lola, middle name Kimiko. So you see, she might as well celebrate the news with someone. No, she's never had children herself, though she would have liked to.

"I've been living here alone since my two sisters died, one ten years ago, the other one last year."

Inside, the house is like any other rural house belonging to an old person: crochet dollies, a smell halfway between potpourri and bin bottom, yellowed photographs on dark wooden furniture. I look at one of them, showing three smiling, well-dressed ladies in their sixties in front of the castle.

"My sisters and me," Adrienne says.

She flicks her key onto a little flower-shaped hook and tells us to make ourselves at home (tricky for the Sun, whose wheelchair is a bit too big to navigate the tiny, cramped living room—way too many coffee tables, chairs and empty boxes). We squeeze onto the sofa around a mangy dog who takes up all the space.

Plop! Goes a bottle somewhere.

"Champagne!" Adrienne says, bringing us five glasses.

"Thank you, but my sister and I don't drink," the Sun tells her.

"Not even fruit juice or something?"

"If you've got fruit juice or something, sure."

She fishes a bottle of fruit juice or something from a cupboard, and pours Astrid and me a glass of champagne each.

"Astrid," I say to my blonde friend, "if you start telling us your most secret fantasies when you're drunk, I solemnly promise to only take note of half of them."

"And if you stand up on the table and show us your knickers, I'll only take three pictures."

"Deal!"

We clink glasses. Astrid, as we already know, has a thing for champagne. I'm not yet used to the taste—a bit too frank, a bit too fizzy, with its bubbles like needles—bitchy, those bubbles, vaguely sneaky, compared with the big booming air pockets of a good old Perrier.

"To Lola!" says the Sun, raising his glass.

"To Lola," the old lady confirms. "Would you mind looking at that thing they bought me, there, the... the *tablet*—would you mind looking to see whether they've sent me any pictures?"

The Sun shows her the half-Japanese great-grand-niece from a variety of angles in the dozen photos taken by the happy parents.

"I don't know why he was always so keen to go to Japan. It was his thing. Then he found a Japanese woman. That said, she's very nice. It's like you," she says to Hakima and the Sun. "You're very nice, even though... even though..."

"Even though we don't drink champagne?"

"Yes. But it's good, it just means there's more for the rest of us..."

We help Adrienne prepare dinner: tagliatelle with courgettes from the garden, frozen burgers, lettuce, also from the garden—which needs to be carefully parted from all its slugs—and supermarket cherry tomatoes. Astrid runs to the trailer to get a few sausages, as a thank-you present to Adrienne.

Meanwhile, we tell her about our lives, our journey, our reasons for it. She thinks it's complicated and stressful.

"That's what society's like, these days... I'd rather be sitting here quietly in my garden. That's what I like about this place: it's out of the way, and calm, and old. The castle hasn't changed since the Renaissance. It won't. The garden, you just need to look after it so it stays the same year in, year out. That's good. Long-lasting."

Astrid comes back and begins to cook the sausages, expertly tossing them around a partly de-Tefloned pan.

"Yet you must have moved around a bit," I note, bringing the open champagne bottle to the table. "You told us you weren't born here."

"Oh, that's true," says Adrienne, "but that... that wasn't the same thing."

The atmosphere is relaxed as we start to eat, sitting around the mahogany table, using blackened silverware that must be a family heirloom. I feel like I've brushed against a potentially interesting, but also sensitive, topic. After another glass of champagne, I go up to second gear. "Where did you and your sisters spend your childhood?"

"Our childhood?" She gulps down some champagne, then a big chunk of bread, which stretches the wrinkly skin of her throat. "In Nevers, a few hours' drive from here."

"Nevers? We're supposed to be cycling there tomorrow. Do you go back often?"

She shakes her head. Never. She hasn't been back since she was sixteen.

"When was that?"

"When I left? In 1945. With my sisters."

Astrid whistles to indicate that 1945 was so long ago that everything was probably in black and white back then—the city must have changed so much since that the lady would find it unrecognizable. She probably remembers woods, fields and little gardens, and now it must be piles of buildings, car parks and supermarkets. Adrienne seems to agree:

"I've never wanted to go back."

"Why did you leave at such a young age?"

It takes some time for our host to reply to this. She spends that time slicing through three different cheeses (Reblochon, Morbier, Cabécou) and drinking another mouthful of champagne.

"Because of my sister Marguerite—we left for her sake."

We pick small home-grown strawberries from a bowl, waiting for the story to come. It finally does.

"She was fifteen, I was sixteen and Lucile, our older sister, was eighteen. We were as naive as the little birds. We had great dreams—we wanted to live together, travel and work together. We weren't even thinking of getting married; come the end of the war—because of course, at the time, we were at war: Nevers was in Nazi-occupied France—come the end of the war we thought we'd go to America and open a shop there."

"But clearly," says Astrid, "it didn't work out that way."

(Astrid, world rubbing-salt-in-the-wound champion.)

"No," Adrienne replies. "Marguerite fell in love with a man in our village. She met with him almost every day in the woods and the countryside. They were, er—good friends."

"Was he in the Resistance or was he a collaborator?" Hakima asks.

"Hakima!" the Sun grumbles.

"Neither," the old lady whispers.

"Not everyone was in the Resistance or a collaborator," Astrid explains in a teacher's voice. "It's a highly simplified vision of what happened in France during the Second World War."

"But they told us at school..."

"That's because you're young. They put it like that so you wouldn't get confused. But when you get to our age, you'll do the Second World War in History again and you'll see it's *much more complicated than that*. That's what Madame Adrienne means: he was neither resisting nor collaborating; he was keeping himself alive, that's all."

Or maybe that's not all. The Sun's onto something: "That good friend of your sister's, was he French?"

"No," says Adrienne, "he wasn't."

"What was he, then?" asks Hakima.

The Sun frowns and whispers something into Hakima's ear.

"Oh," she goes. "That makes me think, we don't know any Germans, do we?... No, we don't."

I do. It's him who doesn't know me.

"So what if he was German?"

"So what? Hakima, France was at war with Germany."

"Oh, right. So they should have killed each other, and instead they were going out. But when you think about it, if everyone had done that, then we wouldn't have needed to be at war or anything. It's like that documentary we saw, remember, where the Jewish and the Palestinian people, you know, they were living together and eating together instead of the Jewish people killing the Palestinians all the time."

The Sun coughs. "Ahem, Hakima, Astrid's right, it's a bit more complicated than that, those things—"

"But you always say the Palestinians keep getting killed by the J—"

"Hakima, please..."

Adrienne nods, but she seems to think it was actually quite simple. It simply meant her little sister could never marry her lover.

She starts again, "At some point, Nevers was bombed."

"By the Germans," Hakima suggests.

"No. By the Allies."

"Who?"

"France's allies."

"What? But why?"

(We're getting to the limits of the Year 8 History curriculum.)

"They were trying to liberate France. But the bombing killed a lot of civilians. Anyway, a few months later, Nevers was liberated."

174

"By the Allies?"

"Yes, by the Allies."

(Hakima smiles, satisfied that this episode at least is understandable.)

"And of course," Adrienne says, "they shot lots of people in the streets."

"They shot who?... Germans?"

"Yes, but also French people who had collaborated with the Germans—or who were suspected of having done so. They shot Marguerite's friend."

"Oh, no!" Hakima moans. "I knew it. I knew it would be a sad story. At least they didn't shoot her—they can't have done because there's a picture of her over there looking all old."

"They didn't, no. They generally didn't do that to women."

But the Sun, Astrid and I know what they did to women.

"Women who'd slept with Germans had their heads shaved," Adrienne mutters. "Afterwards they paraded Marguerite through the village like that, in front of everybody."

She dumps her strawberry stalks and cheese rinds into a small bowl and downs what's left of the champagne, probably rather flat by now.

"And since they thought Lucile and I might have slept with Germans too, they did the same to us."

"What? That's so unfair!" screams Hakima, who's really a good audience for this kind of storytelling. "*You* hadn't done anything wrong!"

"Hakima," the Sun groans, "it was *also* unfair for their other sister. She hadn't done anything wrong either."

Adrienne nods. "We were skinny, bald, humiliated. As soon as we set foot outside, people would hurl insults at us. People we hardly knew cursed us in the most horrible way. We were shamed—all the time. It wasn't easy, you know."

"Yes," pipes Astrid. "We do know."

She's not wrong. It's not the same thing, but we know.

"We locked ourselves underground, in our parents' cellar, waiting for our hair to grow back. It wasn't too bad; we played games together. We grew even closer than before."

"Good strategy," I say. "Strength in unity."

"A year later, we came out again. But people still remembered, and we were still getting abuse thrown at us. We had to go away."

"To America?"

"No, to here. An aunt told us the castle of Longuemort was looking for a couple of wardens. Instead, we offered them a trio of very respectable sisters. They said yes. We settled down and stayed."

"For eighty years?"

"Pretty much. In the end we did spend our lives working together, just as we'd always wanted."

She sinks back into her chair and stares at the chandelier, calmly.

"But not in the real world," murmurs Astrid, being her usual tactful self. "You cut yourselves off from the real world."

"The real world hadn't given us anything we liked. It's not easy to get over such abuse, such humiliation. It's not easy to get over a war. You want to crawl under your bed and never get out again, if you see what I mean."

"I do," says Kader softly.

"The four of you—I've heard your story on TV, you know," says the old lady. "I was very moved by it."

She said those last few words reluctantly, as if she didn't want to admit that she might be moved by anything.

Later, before we go to bed—she offered to let us sleep in her sisters' bedrooms, but that would have been weird, so instead we pitched our tents just outside in the garden—I walk up to her and ask, in an annoyingly shaky voice, "Adrienne, your—your little sister—I was wondering, do you think... do you think he manipulated her? The German, I mean? Do you think—do you think maybe because he was strong and powerful, he impressed her and everything, and he knew he could get—I don't know, maybe food or something—by being with her? You think he was exploiting her?"

"Oh, no. She was in love with him, that's all. He was nice."

"But men take advantage of their power sometimes."

"Yes, that happens. It does."

I visualize that very young girl from Nevers, throwing herself into the arms of her German lover in a field, all in black and white, of course, because it was so long ago. And then the German is shot. And now he's lying in a pool of blood, blood that's streaming from the

177

holes in his uniform. In a black-and-white world, blood is black.

But then again, maybe it *was* wrong, what they did.

Sometimes you just aren't allowed to be together, and that's that.

For example, in France, if a teacher sleeps with a student, the teacher can be sent to prison.

Except that, as Mum's told me a million times, she was twenty-five years old when it happened. At twenty-five, you're well over the age of consent. ("It's not ethical to go out with your students anyway," I said. "Perhaps, but it's not illegal, Miss Know-It-All." "It's not ethical. It's pathetic-al." "Maybe it's not ethical, maybe it's pathetic-al, but you wouldn't be born, Mireille, if I hadn't made that decision at that time.")

What I now know is that when Mum chose to become a high-school teacher in a small provincial town, she wasn't wasting her time. She was *taking* her time. She was taking her time to write a response to Klaus.

Being and Bewilderment: Towards a Philosophy of the Unexpected. I've read it. It goes against Klaus's philosophy.

Klaus thinks human nature is all about planning and mapping. Human beings create programmes, plans, maps, predictions. Human beings are creatures who know there's such a thing as *tomorrow*, and that it needs to be prepared for, predicted, prophesied.

Patricia Laplanche, my mother, thinks the opposite. She writes that what's unique in human nature is that we find joy in surprise, in newness, in the unexpected.

178

Human beings make plans and draw maps, sure—but that's not what makes us human. If anything, that's what makes us animals. Animals plan things too. Bees sculpt honeycombs, cats calculate the trajectory of their paws towards the butterfly they want to catch (except Fluffles, who's a lame butterfly hunter). But human beings are only properly human because they draw novelty and the unexpected from this well-ordered world. Art, emotion and life are what happen when plans, programmes and predictions fail.

Klaus's condom tears, and the unexpected happens: an unexpected little piglet. Me.

Did Mum go to Bourg-en-Bresse to run away from the real world? She never told Klaus she was pregnant by him. They'd already "stopped seeing each other" when she realized. It was almost too late to have an abortion: for a few weeks she just thought she was a little sick, and then she found out she was expecting me. She decided to keep me—why? As a souvenir? No: because she felt she could handle it. It's the only explanation she's ever given me: "I don't know, Mireille, stop nagging me with that. I felt like I could handle it, that's all."

"I think you made the wrong choice. In retrospect, I mean. Seeing what I turned out to be like, personally, I'd have aborted myself."

"Goodness, my dear girl, you can't imagine how much I'm looking forward to the time when you'll stop wallowing in morbid thoughts. For now, you could at least make an effort and dress up as a goth."

179

"But can you believe it? I could, I *should* never have existed. It makes me dizzy just thinking about it."

"Indeed. All those quiet afternoons and evenings I could have had..."

"Don't listen to her, Mireille," says Philippe Dumont, "we'd be bored without you..."

THREE LITTLE PIGLETTES
TROTTING TOWARDS NEVERS

EXCLUSIVE —Mireille Laplanche, the spokesperson for the "Three Little Piglettes", has told our newspaper that the young girls and their now famous sausage trailer will stop for a lunchtime sale in the small town of Cercy-la-Tour in the Nièvre region, before reaching Nevers in the early evening.

Mireille Laplanche, Astrid Blomvall and Hakima Idriss were expected yesterday in Gueugnon, but never made it there, spending the night instead near the castle of Longuemort. "We're a little behind schedule," Laplanche confided, "but we're still planning on being in Paris on the morning of 14th July." The teenagers' journey has triggered an unexpectedly passionate response from bloggers and social-media users; the three friends, who self-define as "piglettes", remain evasive as to what they are intending to do once in Paris for the national holiday, a silence that has been feeding wild speculations on the Internet.

H.L.

Are the Three Little Piglettes just seeking attention, or do they have a good reason for cycling to Paris? Join the conversation on Leprogrès.fr.

The selfie generation! The reality-TV generation! Me, me, me!
Don't give those poor girls the attention they're thirsting after.
Celebrity is a fickle friend!   GillesDeroyLoquart

I must say I am surprised that nobody seems to be questioning
the following: 1) the fact that these very young ladies are selling
sausages, in other words, are working; do they have the required
licence and necessary training? and 2) the potential risks for
them of such a long and arduous journey. All three of them being
extremely obese the possibility of heart attacks is very real.
Permissive parenting endangers children and the rest of society!
                                             AWorriedParent

Whos to say their not about to bomb the Champs-Élysées???!!!
They say they have sausage in their trailer has anyone gone and
check? terrorrists have been using children of that age for ages!
It;s time government did something else than doing nothing!
                                             MarieFrance75

fucking ugly   igor2005

18

"Right, pretty piglettes—and Kader—let's get a move on today. We're slightly behind schedule. We absolutely have to reach the Loire this evening. It's going to be a hard day. Harder than planned."

No, not *harder*—worse.

"Have you seen the forecast? It's not looking good," Adrienne warned us after breakfast, which we ate on the grass, in front of our tents in the castle's garden.

"Oh, the weather gods wouldn't do that to us," I answered, merrily biting a chunk off my buttered baguette. "They've been so sweet so far!"

"Yeah, but that's always how it works," Astrid intervened, full of managerial confidence. "You think it's going to be nice, you sow your seeds, you water your fields, the little shoots start poking through, and suddenly, *whack!* Hailstorm. Half of your harvest—*gone*. It happens all the time in *Farmer IV*."

"Yes, for weirdos like you who like to make things complicated for themselves. In real life, when the sky is cornflower-blue at seven in the morning, it's going to be lovely all day."

Fast-forward an hour and ten minutes, and...

...we're drowning.

It's not just that annoying but manageable kind of rain, which bleaches the landscape and gurgles under your bike wheels. Oh, no. We turn a corner, and it feels like—we've just punched through the skin of a gigantic water-filled balloon.

Everything at ground level is grey-green. The charcoal-coloured cloud ceiling, as fluffy as Fluffles's belly, is so low that the tallest trees seem to be tickling it. Hard to say if the water's falling down from the sky, or rising up towards it. Potholes have turned into muddy marshes, which we try our best to avoid. In front of us, the Sun's skull, shoulders and arms are drenched in water, as slick and shiny as if he were covered in oil. His T-shirt must be completely stuck to his muscular chest, I think, though that fact of course doesn't interest me in the least.

We're soaked: sea sponges. Hakima's normally frizzy hair is plastered to her forehead.

"We're going so slowly," she complains.

"At least we're going."

And at last we burst out the other side of the water balloon. The countryside around us reappears; the huge black ceiling breaks up into dark-grey, kittenish little clouds, which drift lazily apart. The sun, looking a bit pale, reappears behind wispy clouds. We go on bravely—stopping only once, to go to the loo in a small village...

(They're holes in the ground, with broken flushes; there's a huge cone of shit between the two foot rests, around which flies are buzzing so loudly it sounds like they're barking. We end up going in the bushes instead.)

(As formerly hypothesized, the Sun's T-shirt is sticking to his chest. Too bad.)

(Damn, my own T-shirt also seems to be sticking to my chest, and to my belly, and to all the folds and lumps thereof.)

We leave again.

At around 1 p.m., forty-five minutes later than planned, we get to the little town of Cercy-la-Tour, and to the flowery bridge that crosses, so a sign tells us, the River Aron.

"Funny," says Astrid, "I thought it'd be the back of beyond, but look, there must be some kind of funfair going on. There's loads of people on the bridge..."

Loads of people, yes. A travelling circus? Pilgrims on their way to Santiago de Compostela? A local music festival? Oh, they're holding a banner. How convenient; we'll know what it's all about.

The banner's blue, white and red, and it reads:

CERCY WELCOMES THE THREE LITTLE PIGLETTES!!!

They lead us to the banks of the Aron, and bring us...

"Champagne? *Again?*"

And Coke and lemonade and fruit juices, boxes of chocolates, bread, flowers and chips. The mayor of the town is there, as well as those of half a dozen neighbouring towns and villages. We're surrounded by kids who haven't gone away on holiday, by most of Cercy's inhabitants, and by many people who've come from the surrounding area too...

...including, of course, journalists, who have driven all the way from...

"Montceau-les-Mines! We were expecting you yesterday, young ladies!"

"Nevers. I'm a reporter for the local radio..."

"Might you answer a few questions for *Ouest-France*? I came from Nantes this morning..."

"And *we* came from *Paris*, can you imagine! So, Miss Laplanche, you really need to answer our questions..."

"Does the *Bresse Courier* have exclusive access to you?"

"What are you going to do in Paris on 14th July?"

("Shose shaushages are sho good!")

"What do your parents think of this strange adventure?"

"LADIES AND GENTLEMEN!" the mayor of Cercy booms. "Leave these young ladies alone!"

Actually, these young ladies don't mind the attention. Astrid dishes out sauce like an expert dinner lady; Hakima takes orders, leaping this way and that to grab cardboard plates and plastic cutlery—and meanwhile, I watch the sausages, which give off a satisfying sizzle as they fry.

Then we allow ourselves a break to eat something, on the riverbank.

They want us to try everything, and everything's delicious. Even the Coke in a plastic cup is delicious.

The buttered bread is delicious. The dry *saucisson* with hazelnuts; those tiny barbecued fish from the river; the huge salad that someone brought along—lentils, tomatoes, grated carrots, sunflower seeds, all energetically tossed together; the olive oil—oh God! It's scented with truffles!—drizzled over hungrily torn hunks of bread; those shiny little mounds of yoghurt that seem to be bleeding raspberry coulis; those baskets of gleaming chocolates and pralines, already beginning to melt...

"Are you sure you don't want a glass of champagne?"

"No, thanks—we've still got a lot of cycling to do, you know..."

"And *we* were supposed to feed you, not the other way around!" Astrid protests, her mouth full of tapenade.

"It's our pleasure!"

We've also attracted a small group of—for want of a better word—fans. One of them seems very proud to be able to tell us that he knows the person who created the Facebook group "Where are the Three Little Piglettes?", which attempts to map our journey. The others are equally keen to take part in the Quest, and enthusiastically speculate as to why and how we've undertaken our fascinating trip. There are about a dozen of them, aged from twenty to forty, huddled in a corner and looking awkward.

"Course, as I'm sure you can guess, we all have our theories," a young man tells us, avoiding our eyes. "Personally, I think you're trying to warn the president about the Bresse chickens."

"About the Bresse chickens?"

"Yes." (Talking in a very low voice now.) "As soon as I heard you were from Bourg-en-Bresse, I *knew*. Gamma rays in poultry. Health scandal. Irradiated chickens, a rise in cases of cancer among consumers. You know the truth, and you're going to tell the president."

"What gamma rays? What cancer?"

"Sshh," the weird guy whispers. "Don't say it too loudly just yet."

He pats our backs, murmuring, "You're very brave."

Then we sign autographs.

I repeat: *we sign autographs*.

"But I don't have a signature!" Hakima panics. "I've never had one!"

People are mostly getting us to sign newspaper articles, and that's when we start to realize how big we've become. At least eight different national newspapers have written about us today. We're on the front page of *Aujourd'hui en France*.

"Urgh, it's the grossest photo in the world!" Astrid complains. "You're lucky, Mireille, at least your head is tilted down."

The four of us, seen from the front, on the road: the Sun, divinely handsome, looking like a modern Ben-Hur; behind him, the Three Little Piglettes, whose physical efforts aren't quite as graceful.

"Who took that picture? How come we didn't see them?"

According to the credit below the photo, it was taken by a certain René Hogue. The article it accompanies is... suspiciously precise. They know that my mother is a philosophy teacher in Bourg. They know Astrid is half-Swedish. They know—oh, how interesting—they know that Kader Idriss is currently at the heart of an internal army inquest...

In fact, the Sun, is attracting more attention today than before, at least from the shrewder journalists.

"Monsieur Idriss, there are a lot of theories surrounding your participation in this trip. Some people are speculating that the 'Three Little Piglettes' might be a red herring, and that *you*'re the real reason for this odyssey. Are you intending to disturb the Bastille Day military parade in order to defend your version of what happened when your unit was ambushed?"

The Sun, brightly, haughtily: "I'm here to be with my young sister and to look after her and her friends. It's also a physical challenge for me, to get used to my new body. I have no intention whatsoever of doing anything that would stain the honour of the French Army, in which I would still be a soldier if it were up to me. That will be all, thank you."

We hop back on our saddles having eaten way too much, our eyes prickling with sleepiness.

"Right. Focus. We've still got a long way to go. A long way."

The journalists' motorbikes tail us. Some of the geeks are following us by car (I hope the nuclear-Bresse-chicken conspiracy theorist isn't among them). The weather is still good, but it's starting to smell like rain...

"My belly's hurting," Hakima says. "It's like it's full of gravel... scraping and scratching everything inside."

"It's clots," I explain. "Big blobs of blood."

"I want to cry," Hakima says.

"It's really painful, we know," says Astrid, "we feel for you, love. Have you taken another ibuprofen?"

"No, I don't want to get used to it or else it won't work any more."

"Of course it'll work, it's not like antibiotics!"

"Are you sure?"

"Sure! I've been taking ibuprofen for years, I had precocious puberty."

"You had precocious puberty, Astrid?"

"Yeah, I was eight and a half."

"Christ! Eight and a half?"

"Yes, I already had boobs and hips and periods... it was horrible, I couldn't go to the swimming pool."

"Oh wow, that's awful—poor you!"

"It *was* awful. I'd lock myself up in my bedroom and listen to Indochine on a loop. You know, Hakima, you should take some ibuprofen. You'll take ibuprofen your whole life anyway, because of periods, or migraines, or something—you'll almost always be aching somewhere, it's flipping annoying being a girl."

The Sun, gentleman that he is, pretends not to hear.

The road is so, so, so, so long...

...but we finally get to Nevers, under a cool, thin rain,

exhausted, shattered, drained, and of course there's a welcoming committee; I'm probably going to throw up, or maybe even die, who knows? Good evening, ladies and gentlemen, what kind of sausage would you like? No, no, we're not doing any interviews until later, sir. Let us sell our sausages.

19

In Nevers, the night is cold and Astrid is snoring.

Despite being tired, I can't sleep. I stare straight up at the ceiling of the tent and the two bits of string that dangle in the middle of it (what are those bits of string for, anyway?). Light from the moon, or perhaps, more plausibly, from a lamp, daubs the fabric white. Through it, I can see the dancing silhouettes of dozens of little mosquitoes and an occasional clumsy moth.

I slip out of the tent silently. The campsite is dark, but it's only midnight and some tents are still lit, looking like big Chinese lanterns on the black grass. You can see the shadows of the people inside, including a couple looking very much like they're in the middle of *doing it*. You'd really have to be a bit of a flasher to do that, or stupid enough not to realize that people outside can see everything, right down to the turned-up nose and half-open mouth of the girl who's sitting on top of the guy. Surely that must hurt your knees a bit? Of course, it depends how long it's going to last, but can you imagine the state of your kneecaps after just five minutes of that posi—

"Everything OK, Mireille?"

I jump and turn around to face the Sun, in his chariot, on the gravel path that leads to the building at the centre of the campsite. His face is lit up from below by the white glow of his iPhone; it looks exhausted, almost like a death mask.

"Hey! Kader! What's up? Yep, all good, perfect, great!"

"You looked puzzled."

"No, no, I was just wondering something about a thing."

"Can I help?"

"Ha! No. Not at all. It's absolutely zero per cent important. It's about..." (SOS. Don't say anything about any sexual position whatsoever.) "It's about that little string that dangles at the top of the tent. What's that thing for, anyway?"

"For hanging things from. Like a lamp, for example."

"Oh! Of course! Yes! Makes complete sense!" I slam my hand on my forehead, rather forcefully. "It'd been nagging at me for a while. You aren't asleep?"

"No, I was just going to take a walk. Well, you get my meaning."

I walk up to him (it's dark—I can get away with blushing, as long as he can't feel the heat from my burning ears).

I realize that he's breathing quickly and shallowly.

"So... you're just, erm, taking a walk in the middle of the night?"

He propels himself forward slightly, and I can tell he's stifling a groan. "Yeah, why? What's the problem?"

"Nothing."

"Right. See you tomorrow then. Goodnight."

He starts off again, sighs deeply, wipes his brow. In the light from his phone I see a necklace of sweat across his collarbones. I crouch down closer to him to see his face better—it's as waxy and creviced as the surface of the moon.

"You OK, Kader?"

"Fine. But you—you're going to catch a cold. Goodnight."

He scratches my head like I'm his cat or his daughter (I suddenly remember I haven't washed my hair in two days and have a horrifying vision of the oil from my skull accumulating under his nails). He wheels himself forward a few yards. Something falls off the wheelchair; he doesn't notice—he keeps dragging himself along the path.

I call out to him: "Hey, Kader, you dropped your—your washbag."

He turns his head towards me and his eyes—two white discs in a face liquid with sweat—scare me a little. I stammer, "Are you going to have a shower? I'll come with you, if you want."

Oh, perfect. I have just proposed to the Sun that I take a shower with him. I burst out into a frantic cackle. "But not to have a shower myself, right! I've already had a shower! I'm not going to have two showers in one evening! That would be completely absurd! And a total waste of water when thousands of polar bears are dropping dead every minute!"

194

(*Darling, if you keep bleating like that, you'll wake up the whole campsite.*)

"But I could... I don't know, help you. If you need help, that is. I'll cover my ears and my eyes."

That makes him laugh, and clench his teeth, and groan, and I wonder if the moonlight is going to make the Sun turn into a muscly werewolf right in front of me; but at last he says, "OK. Thanks."

It's one of those moments where your existence, which until now has been wandering aimlessly, suddenly slams back into itself with an elastic *slap*. Reality yells into my ears: *He wants me to help him.* He wants me to push his wheelchair along the path towards the main building of the campsite, a huge, ugly cube, swarming with tiny flies.

The neon lamps in the showers fizzle and tinkle when I flick them on, and the harsh light wakes up the resident fauna. Small slugs are slogging up the walls. Gigantic mosquitoes, puppet-clumsy, bounce against the taps and fall to their gooey deaths into puddles of soap. There's a hedgehog in one of the showers. A *hedgehog*.

Camping rule number one: never have a shower in the middle of the night. It's no time for humans.

In the slippery light reflected by the dirty mirrors, I watch myself pushing the Sun's chariot. We both look wilted, pasty.

"Shouldn't you have gone sooner?"

"I don't like it when there's—*gnnnn*—people around."

"Blimey, Kader, are you sure you're OK?"

"Yeah—can you park me in the furthest shower, please?"

It's the disabled shower. I swing the door open and push the chair near the whitish wall, which is spattered with icky soap streaks. In one swift move, the Sun pops out of his chair, catches the bar, sits down on the little stool, and takes his T-shirt off. There's time for me to notice his contracting triceps, his tile-like abs, his pecs like twin tortoise shells. But in this setting, the shower walls covered in grimy tiles, the plughole furry with human hair, there's nothing at all electrifying about this muscle show.

A moment later, and he's taken off his trousers. No, not taken off—ripped off. No need to close your eyes, Mireille—he's wearing underpants. You've seen men like that at the swimming pool. No need to close your eyes.

The men at the swimming pool had legs, though, not stumps.

Head down, Kader breathes jerkily, gulping for air, stifling swear words and whimpers of pain like he's just burnt himself.

"You OK, Kader?"

I've officially become The Amazing "You OK, Kader?" Whispering Automaton. *Youokkader? Youokkader?* Arms hanging by my sides, I watch him huff and grunt, not sure what to do. His left leg has been amputated well above the knee, the right one just above it. Both ends are round, the colour of wood and flame, red-raw, as if they're burning from the inside.

"You OK, Kader?" (Oh, bloody hell.) "What's wrong?"

"Nothing. It's normal. Pass me my washbag, please."

I do. Then, not really thinking about what I'm doing, I take the shower head, flick the tap on, check the temperature. Weird thoughts come into my head that have no place in this situation, at this time. In a daydream I see myself as Fireman Sam, putting out the flames in Kader's legs, our brightly coloured playdough bodies reflected in each tile on the wall. Kader is pale and shaking. I start dousing him in water, with the careful, disciplined concentration of a little girl doing her homework. There's a puncture in the hose that snakes from the wall to the shower head; two little jets of water spray out on either side.

"It's OK, you can stop now," Kader whistles between his teeth. "Hand me that... towel."

He wipes himself dry, slowly, leaving his two scalding stumps till last and patting them very softly. Then he sits up, shakes his still-wet hair, and gets a tube of cream out of his bag.

"It's sweat," he says in an almost-normal voice now. "And all the rubbing. The skin isn't the same as everywhere else, there, it gets inflamed easily. You get things, eczema, all sorts of stuff like that. Ideally, you should..." He falls silent, and lathers some cream on his left leg. "You should do this every day, but since we set off it's been worse, because of all the sweat."

Once he's worked in the cream, his stumps are as pink and gleaming as a baby's skin. He tips some snow-white powder onto them. I come up with a revolutionary variation on "You OK, Kader?":

"You better now, Kader?"

"Hmm. There's a clean T-shirt in my bag and my pyjama bottoms are there too."

I hand them to him and help him slip on his T-shirt. Now he's clean and warm and smells soapy-sweet. He sits back into his chair, and I wrap my hands around the handles.

"You could have, I don't know, you could have told us, we'd have helped."

"It's OK, I can do it on my own, usually. It's just that campsites are tricky. I'd rather there wasn't anyone around."

"Yeah, I know how you feel. It's like when I go for a swim, I'd rather be alone. Though *you're* fine—I mean, you don't look bad."

"You don't either," he chuckles.

He's a very nice man.

"So have you been doing that alone ever since we set off?"

"I couldn't the first night, because there weren't any showers anywhere. Yesterday, Adrienne's bathroom was crazy—there were potpourri bowls all around the bath."

"Oh yeah, I remember! That was bizarre. And that petrified sea sponge, on the left, did you see that?"

"Aaaah, so *that's* what was poking my arse! I thought it was a cushion, but it turned out to be so fucking stiff."

"You bet, it's a skeleton."

"Old people are so weird."

This more relaxed conversation leads us back to the path.

"Thanks, by the way," the Sun says.

"No problem. You're welcome."

"I know it's gross."

"It's not gross, it's nature."

"No, it's not. It's medicine. If it was nature, I'd be dead. There's no room in nature for an amputee."

My turn to ruffle his hair (tonight, I can do anything). It's thin, damp and tangled, algae-like. *Don't worry, Kader,* I think, *there's plenty of room in my heart for an amputee.* Instead, I tell him, "Well, what's left of you is beautiful."

That makes him laugh.

We get closer to the tents... and I notice something far away, barely visible in the darkness of the campsite: a silhouette walking towards our stuff.

"Look, someone's checking out our trailer."

"Must be a fan wanting to take a picture."

"In the middle of the night? Bit of a silly thing to do."

A square of light: the silhouette is leaning over our bikes, lighting them up with his phone.

"Oh, he's trying to see what make they are, I think. He's going to be disappointed, poor guy, if he's hoping they're any good..."

The *poor guy* stays there for a while. He's far away; we can't see what he's doing. Bats are shrieking and bickering in the dark-brown sky.

"I'm going to ask him what he wants," the Sun says.

We start on our way. "You know, Kader, I think he just heard that we were staying at this campsite, and..."

What's that noise?

Not the bats, not the cicadas, not the snoring from the other tents—no. More like the noise of a balloon slowly deflating.

Or a *tyre*.

"Shit! What the?..."

The guy's spotted us—he gets up, runs off. Campsite crime! Just like in a horror film, I see—I swear it's true—a sliver of moonlight reflected from a knife blade.

The Sun's already some way ahead of me, his wheelchair zigzagging between the tents, bouncing over the bumps on the ground, chasing the sprinting shadow towards the gate of the campsite.

Meanwhile, I check our bikes. Damn it! That bastard's knifed five tyres out of six, and snipped all the brake cables.

That bastard, the Sun informs me furiously when he comes back, jumped over the fence of the campsite and vanished. And if he had legs, damn it, if only he had legs, he'd have followed him...

"But who *was* it?"

"Who do you *think*? I saw him clear as day in the light of the lamp by the gate. Easy to recognize, with his bloody stupid haircut. It's your Pig Pageant guy."

BR(E)AKING NEWS:
THREE LITTLE PIGLETTES' BIKES SABOTAGED

Mireille Laplanche, the spokesperson of the now famous trio, the "Three Little Piglettes", has told our newspaper that the teenagers' trip is likely to be delayed. This morning, the young women found their bike tyres slashed and their brake cables cut, in what seems to be an act of vandalism.

Three bike shops in Nevers have spontaneously offered the girls their assistance. The campsite where the teenagers were staying is currently analysing the tapes from their CCTV cameras. "We will be in Paris on 14th July," Mireille Laplanche assured us. The team had factored some time into their schedule for delays due to unforeseen circumstances.

H.L.

Simone Suffragette @simonesuffragette
Solidarity with #3littlepiglettes whose bikes were sabotaged last night in Nevers!
291 retweets

Zara Belle @zarabelle
You'd have to be such a dickhead to do something like that #justice #3littlepiglettes

Camping Nevers @campingnevers
Deepest apologies to #3littlepiglettes for V. UNCOMMON intrusion in our highly rated campsite 1/2

Camping Nevers @campingnevers
#3littlepiglettes were given free night and investigations are ongoing. Security normally exemplary 2/2

City of Paris @cityofparis
Mayor of Paris Élise Michon wishes to express her support to #3littlepiglettes. Safe trip to #Paris!
3,021 retweets

20

"*An Ode to Gaston, Zoltan and Philou,*
Bike Mechanics in Nevers."

by Mireille Laplanche, emergency poet

Some say the world will end in fire,
Some say in ice.
I'm more concerned by slashed-up tyres
And snipped, dangling brake wires.
But all's well now! The super-nice
Gaston, Zoltan and you, Philou,
Have saved our lives by giving us
Shiny new wheels, and brakes, brand new!
New saddles too! What lucky lasses,
We'll no longer have such painful—

"No, Mireille, honestly, it's not in the best of taste. Especially as that poem is already profoundly idiotic..."

"I'd like to see you write an ode to our saviours, Miss *Kitchen Rush*! I don't think you've got any high scores for iambic-pentameter management."

"I don't even know why you're sending them a poem, it's a moronic idea."

"It's the only way of thanking them from the bottom of our hearts."

"We gave them loads of sausages!"

"Unlike yours, dear Astrid, the bottom of my heart isn't layered with sausages. Right, then how about this:

With lightened hearts and lightened trailer,
We leave your town and swear that never;
No, never! Ever, ever, ever,
Will we forget you three or Nevers.

"*Never* doesn't rhyme with *Nevers*."

"You don't know anything about poetry, which is entirely to be expected, since you're a fan of Indochine. Here we go—slap a stamp on, and in the postbox it goes."

"Are you done yet?" shouts Hakima, getting impatient on her bike.

"Yes, yes, coming!"

Now our bums bounce bountifully on new, gel-filled saddles. Our new tyres, much thicker than the previous ones, howl with laughter as they steamroll through pebbles, potholes and notches in the road. Ecstasy!

And best of all, the three mechanics have replaced our home-made trailer-towing system. In retrospect, it feels like we'd been dragging a delivery truck up until now. Gaston, Zoltan and Philou have made us a bespoke new harness. As they explained, it distributes our pulling forces equally over the whole trailer, which is now gloriously responsive. Zoltan, in a stroke of genius, has also installed a special brake on the trailer, controlled by me—we can now slow down with no risk of being bulldozed.

"Hello, Hélène? It's Mireille... You can't hear me very well? That's cos I'm on my hands-free... Yeah, we're off again. Just to update you on the situation—everything's going well, in fact, we're much *better* now. You can write that as big as you like on the *Bresse Courier* website: the guy who did this to us has miserably failed at being a terrorist. Yes, we're going much faster now. We think we'll get to Sancerre around 2 p.m. We should be able to make up the time we've lost... You'll write that, OK? *Not only will that evil vandal burn in hell, he can also tell himself he's the laughing stock of all self-respecting criminals.* Yeah, sure, you can quote me, no problem. Hey, piglettes! It's Hélène—say hi!"

"Hi!"

The road running along the banks of the River Loire is a shock of white and quiet, disturbed only by the occasional jogger. Hakima and Astrid are counting birds. Herons with Mohicans and curved necks amble on triangles of sand in the middle of the river; ducks, some of them followed by kiwi-fruit-sized ducklings, waddle near fishermen; sparrows dive under our wheels, apparently just for the frisson of a near-death experience; crows pinch bits of leftover sandwiches from bins. Many people recognize us now, but by the time they've pulled out their phones to take a picture, we're already gone.

"It's as if we're getting more and more famous," Hakima observes.

This morning, the Sun, Astrid and I had a long, adult conversation, during which we decided to hide the size of the media buzz from Hakima. We haven't told her that the mayor of Paris, as well as several deputies and senators and influential journalists, have tweeted that they *can't wait* to see us in Paris. We haven't told her that Simone Suffragette has written a column in *Libération* about us. We haven't told her that the cars and motor-bikes following us at a distance are probably filming us for some 24/7 news channel.

We haven't told her all that, not because we're worried it might make her conceited, but because every time someone says we're amazing, strong, smart and admirable, somebody else, on some social network, somewhere, is writing that we're repulsive fat cows, dogs, pigs, whores, sluts, bitches, hags, butt-ugly slags.

Who are those people? It's a mystery. Are there actually real people—real, living, laughing and dancing people— behind those appalling insults?

Astrid's fine; she's started taking it all very philosoph-ically. And of course I attained ultimate wisdom a long time ago and am no longer hurt by such things. But it's true that, once in a while, a particularly sour comment, a particularly well-aimed, particularly cruel one, makes my self-confidence crumble. For instance, that one on the website of *Le Monde*: "Those three young girls are pitiful. Poor Mireille especially, who seems convinced she's very clever, when in fact she's stupid as well as ugly. Shameful to let those kids strut around on national TV." Another, anonymous one, on the *Bresse Courier* website: "I go to school with Mireille Laplanche. She's manipulative and sucks up to teachers."

It's not always the *fat pigs* and *you're fucking ugly* comments that punch holes through your throat.

The Sun: "Stop reading the comments, Mireille, or I'm taking that phone away from you."

That's precisely why we've decided to conceal the truth from Hakima: if even *I* find it difficult to get over those comments, then Hakima, Hakima... We just can't do that to her.

So we're pedalling. This morning, I asked the Sun: "Youokkader?" and he said: "Yep, all OK, Mireille." I didn't see any signs of pain on his face as he started to push himself along.

The banks of the Loire are great for cycling. You can't always see the river, but you feel its slumbering presence behind the trees. We're on a cycle path, so the journalists with their cars and mopeds are leaving us alone. There aren't many ups or downs to the route, and the sky gods have decided to stop messing us about: for the first time, it feels like we're eating up the miles calmly, painlessly. The soreness of the first couple of days has faded into a kind of *entente cordiale* between brain and nervous system: no pain, in exchange for no sensation. Our calves are rubber-ball-hard, almost numb. We're turning into real cyclists—patient machines, cold and stoic.

"But seriously," says the Sun, "if I could get my hands on that bastard... What's his stupid name, again?"

"Malo," I murmur between my teeth.

"Bastard. Do you think he's following us?"

"I don't know. I don't get why he's doing this to us. What does he care? It's not about him."

"It's psychological," Astrid explains. "He wants us humiliated and he hates it that we're suddenly popular."

She's probably right—but to the extent that he'd come and sabotage our bikes? How did he even trek all the way up to us? On his Vespa? From Bourg? I try not to think about it—that's what he'd want me to do. He wants us to be disturbed, confused, stressed. Instead, we're staying focused.

Gling! Gling! Some other cyclists have recognized us and ring their bells...

"Hello, Piglettes!"

"Well done, Piglettes!"

"Hang on in there, Piglettes!"

"You all right, Piglettes?"

"You're the best! Carry on!"

Yes, real people who exist all seem to like us. There's such a gap between the words we read on the Internet and those we hear from people we meet! And it's weird, this popularity. I'm not used to being smiled at like this. I'm not used to being asked how I am. Maybe this is what it feels like to be beautiful—I've always noticed that beautiful people attract all the smiles and all the *Hey, you all rights*. We don't like to see beautiful people not being all right. Ugly people, though—of course they're not all right, they're ugly.

But now, at last, it's like we've earned the right to be asked if we're all right—and to be smiled at.

"Dear piglettes, dear chaperone, Sancerre is coming up ahead!"

"Where?"

"Right here!"

"Right here? You mean right *there*? On that hill?"

"Yep. Beautiful, eh? Gorgeous. I looked it up on Google Earth. You'll see, it's well worth the detour. The castle at the top used to be part of the fortress of—"

"Mireille, it's super far! And it's crazily high up!"

"Astrid, Astrid, always exaggerating. A micro-molehill."

"But why are you so set on going up there?"

"You'll see, Hakima, you'll see..."

"Welcome to our beautiful town of Sancerre, young ladies! The internationally renowned capital of Sancerre wine, and of—"

"Crottin de Chavignol!"

"That's right, Miss Laplanche. I can tell you've been paying attention in Cheese Geography class!" says the mayor, shaking my hand.

"Mireille, did you make us climb all the way up here just to visit the village that makes your favourite cheese?"

"Dearest Scandinavian piglette, we couldn't have missed it. Impossible."

"But Crottin de Chavignol is available *everywhere* in this country! What difference does it make to eat it here?"

"It's like a pilgrimage for me, Astrid. I would ask you to please respect my religious beliefs."

While Astrid and Hakima sulk in a corner, throwing dark glances at me—girls! Always saying mean things to other girls about other girls, that's all girls do—I wait patiently for the heavenly delicacy to be brought to me. As I'd hoped, a young man soon walks up to us, bearing a large pyramid of white crottins... and another young man, with some bread... and while Astrid and Hakima are selling sausages to delegations from the whole region, and while the Sun's busy saying "No, thank you, it's very kind of you but I don't drink" to a pretty young woman who tries to fill his glass with white wine, I'm in my own personal heaven, chatting to the mayor, under the watchful eyes of two cameras (our clingy burrs from BFM TV, and two new journalists from France 3).

Me: "I must tell you, Madame, that I have been a fan of Crottin de Chavignol my whole life. Quite simply, at the age of two and a half months, I shunned the maternal breast and never accepted another drop of milk that hadn't been turned into Crottin de Chavignol."

"Well, you're in the right place. If you want, we'll take you to see where they make the cheese, and introduce you to—"

"Please don't tempt me! We have to be in Briare tonight. We must leave post-haste. But if I'm ever back here, you'll take me?"

"Happily!"

"Even when I'm not famous any more?"

"I doubt you'll remain anonymous for long, Miss Laplanche…"

I blush, and start stuffing my face again, sampling (and by that I mean wolfing down) crottins at different stages of maturity—oh! the powdery bitterness of an old crottin; oh! the moist sourness of a young crottin! Journalists ask me questions to which I give half-answers. Who do you think sabotaged your bikes? A Malovolent person. What are you going to do in Paris on 14th July? Does it have anything to do with the parade? With the fireworks? With the taking of the Bastille? Mireille, you are impressively mature for your age; how come?

"I don't know. Maybe ugliness makes you wiser."

BFM TV @bfm_tv
Spokesperson of #3littlepiglettes Mireille, 15: "Ugliness makes you wiser"
4,910 retweets

Madmoizelle @madmoizelle
"Ugliness makes you wiser" #3littlepiglettes—yes! Let's free ourselves from the cult of beauty!

A.-C. Hussy @Gender!
How about the hashtag #UglyButWise... tell your stories!
#3littlepiglettes

Alex Laurentin @alexlaurentin
I was an ugly teen so now I don't judge people on what they look like #UglyButWise #3littlepiglettes

Yannick Sermonneau @yannick1993
Easy to be seduced by a face, even better to be seduced by a mind #UglyButWise #3littlepiglettes

Since our lives are now an endless chain of firsts, we receive our first offer of branded T-shirts.

Advertising a brand of mass-produced pork products for supermarkets.

"We're launching a new range of sausages," explains the PR person, a very Parisian lady in high heels, holding a stack of T-shirts.

"Good for you, but we're selling Raymond's home-made sausages from the Bourg-en-Bresse market, not plasticky stuff from your factories!"

"There would be financial compensation, of course, which we can discuss away from prying eyes..."

The Sun, like a god of justice, lowers his powerful hand between me and the charcuterie PR. "I'm sorry, Madame. As the guardian of these young women, I cannot allow them to be used as living billboards."

This decision, I'm sure, will be noticed and widely

discussed. No doubt tonight we'll be reading the latest comments on the superb NO we gave to the mass-produced food industry, and on our support for High Quality French Products. ("Miss Laplanche, is your bike trip a way of drawing attention to the exceptional food of our regions?")

"I'm tired, Mireille, I'm hot. Can we go?"

"Yes, Hakima, we'll go soon."

"It's... It's bleeding a lot, today."

"I know. It'll pass."

I squeeze her in my arms like the ninny I am.

We leave again, under whimsical rain, the kind that can't decide if it wants to be a huge downpour or a delicate drizzle when it grows up. It seems to come from nowhere, out of a cloudless sky; I start suspecting that a secret enemy might be following us on the other side of the hedge, aiming a giant shower head at us. Yet, every ten minutes or so, when the fat drops turn to spit, we find ourselves cycling through blinding, psychedelic rainbows, painted by celestial artists with extremely bad taste.

Mireille, we saw you on TV. Answer my texts more than once a day, please. I hope you didn't drink any Sancerre? Call me back. Mum.

Mummy darling whom I will love eternally and for ever, I promise I didn't drink any sincere. Yours Sancerrely xxx

Hi Mireille. Your mother's furious, but you're making me laugh! Miss you. Philippe.

While pedalling, I think of Philippe Dumont, who really is as nice as egg-fried rice. Well, let's not delude ourselves: he's probably just buttering me up so I'll give my huge bedroom to his official son when the little bugger's born. His son, his real, legitimate baby of spectacular beauty. "Mireille, you don't mind sleeping in the cupboard under the stairs from now on, so Julius-Aurelian can have your bedroom, do you? You've always wanted to live like Harry Potter!"

If he tries anything like that...

But actually, I don't think he will. He's been nice to me for years, in exchange for nothing. For years he's been giving me presents that I throw away or break. Why does he do all that, when I'm a cuckoo, a troll, an undesired, undesirable daughter, spoiling his picture-perfect Hollywood happiness, a garden gnome in his Garden of Eden? Philippe Dumont is a strange man.

I don't know if it's euphoria from the endorphins finally kicking in, but we're all on top form this afternoon. Astrid's chatting with Hakima over my shoulder—telling her convent anecdotes, from when she was in Switzerland...

"...so we followed her for two hours through the streets, and then we saw her go into the captain's mansion! She was having a—an affair with him! Can you believe it? A widower, with seven children!"

Hakima is so horrified that she lets go of the handlebars and claps her hands to her mouth.

"What happened next?"

"She broke her vows and left the convent. We all went to the wedding."

"Ah, phew, a happy ending."

Hakima likes stories with happy endings. Luckily, Astrid knows loads of them. The one about the puppy she was looking after, who ran away into the mountains, but was found safe and sound the same evening. The time her arch-enemy stole her diary, but it was locked and she couldn't open it. The time her dad went back to Sweden and abandoned her, but then she discovered Indochine the next week and listened to the songs fifty times over until she knew them by heart and could play them to herself in her head before falling asleep.

"They're not quite the same, though," Hakima cautiously objects. "Indochine and a father."

"Yeah, that's true, Indochine are better most of the time," Astrid answers categorically. "At least Indochine talk to me."

Phew, Hakima's relieved: Astrid's life is much happier with Indochine than with her dad—all's well that ends well. Once again.

How about you, *hypocrite reader*?

How would you like our adventure to end? Would you like Malo to burn our trailer? Would you like us never to reach Paris? Would you like us punished for being fat and ugly? Or are you a tender-hearted, sensitive little soul? Maybe you're hoping for my real dad to kneel down before me and say, "Please forgive me, Mireille, adorable piglette

215

of mine! I never answered your letters, but I think of you every day—here are your half-brothers, Huey, Dewey and Louie—let them give you the kiss of peace!"

What would you rather happened, reader?

While we're on the subject of half-brothers, Huey tweeted something nice about us. What a gentleman. Twenty-three years old, and he's unknowingly expressed support for his secret half-sister. If he only knew! If he only knew! I looked at his face in the little square next to his Twitter handle. He hasn't inherited his father's ugliness: he looks more like his mother, with his black, curly hair. Tortoiseshell glasses, prestigious Parisian high school, now a Political Science student at an elite university.

I don't think I'd like to go to a prestigious Parisian high school and then be a Political Science student at an elite university. I wouldn't have any time to stroke Fluffles and write rubbish poems; plus I'd always have to be either working or going out with the children of other important people. No, I'm better off where I am now.

There's something hypnotic, calming, about the road unrolling under my eyes. My front wheel slices it in two, confidently.

When I see you, Klaus, will I ask you if I can bring my toothbrush and pyjamas to the Élysée Palace and start going to a prestigious Parisian high school, too, just to see what it's like? I'm top of my class, after all. "Mireille will go far."

Yes, but what about Fluffles? And Mum, and Julius-Aurelian? And Philippe Dumont? Klaus, Klaus, you can't ask me to leave them alone in Bourg-en-Bresse. And what about the Georges & Georgette, and that beautiful cushion of beef, the *filet Pierre*?

And Astrid and Hakima, and the Sun? Who'll put out his solar flares, if I'm not there? He can't keep doing it alone his whole life!

I'm not sure what I want my meeting with Klaus to achieve.

Now it's Hakima who's telling Astrid about her life. She never tells *me* anything about her life. She's afraid of Mireille. Mireille pricks up an ear.

"...because, you see, I was very shy. But like, horribly shy, you know, not *normally* shy. Like, I couldn't say hello, or thank you, or goodbye—I couldn't even go into a bakery with my mum! I'd cry if people looked at me. Once, someone on the bus told me my shoelace was undone, and then I cried for two hours."

"That's terrible, poor you! Until when?"

"Until about two years ago."

"But how did you manage to stop being so shy?"

Hakima hesitates, perhaps because the Sun has briefly turned his head towards her. Then she says, "I went to see a child psychologist."

"Oh, really? And it worked?"

"Yeah, but it took time. At the beginning, I couldn't even say a word. I was sitting on my chair like *that*—I couldn't move, I was so scared. She waited for weeks for me to say something. Dad was like, 'We're paying the psychologist 100 euros an hour for Hakima to just sit there and say nothing!' He couldn't understand why Mum wanted me to go. But then I started to relax."

"And what happened? Did she ask you to remember things from when you were a baby? A huge trauma? Had you, like, witnessed a murder or something?"

"No. That's just how I was, that's all. She gave me exercises to do. First we'd go to the supermarket together and I had to say hello to the lady at the till. Then we'd walk in the street and I had to ask somebody the time. Then I had to call restaurants on the phone to book tables. Every time, I cried, I panicked, and then after a few times it would get better. Once, she even made me ring the neighbour's doorbell to borrow some butter—that was horrible."

"But it worked. Now, you're completely fine."

"Yeah. Well... no. I still don't like it when there's loads of people. I don't like talking to people I don't know. I have strategies that the psychologist gave me, like imagining I'm talking to Kader or to Mum instead of the person in front of me. But I don't like it when there's loads of people, I just don't, and when people I don't know come to talk to me."

"But, Hakima," says Astrid, "for the past three days, lots of people we don't know have come to talk to us!"

"I know," says Hakima sadly. "I don't like that at all. Right now, we're cycling, so it's fine, but I know we're going to be in Paris soon, and I've got, like, a knot in my stomach, cos I'm so scared..."

"What? But why haven't you said anything?"

"I don't want to be a bother—"

"You're doing great, darling," the Sun interrupts. "I can tell you're much better, now. It's got nothing to do with that psychologist; it's because you're becoming a strong, confident young woman."

Clearly, the Sun doesn't like psychologists. Maybe he thinks, like his father, that problems like that just disappear when you stop being a pansy about them and decide to be a grown-up. Has *he* ever seen a psychologist? I doubt it. Soldiers don't go to see psychologists. Their stumps might be on fire, sure; but their minds are cool, imperturbable.

It's already dusk by the time we get to Briare. No matter; people are waiting to greet us. I don't even know who they are, probably another mayor, and maybe that guy over there in a suit is a member of parliament. We sell our sausages to people who are absolutely delighted: "We're absolutely delighted to meet you, young ladies"; "I'm delighted to hear it, Madame"; "No, no, it's my pleasure. Our sausages are delicious, the trailer is a delight to look at, and you too, young ladies, are delightful!"

That's overstating it a bit—but I have to admit that we've caramelized nicely under the sun. Astrid's hair is the colour of Sancerre. Her nose is a little burnt, but the rest of her body is a light chestnut, and new freckles hide her pimples. Hakima's skin is almost darker than her hair, which has lightened to sandy-brown. The Sun is more scintillatingly handsome than ever in his wheelchair. And I'm a bit darker too—funny how a slight tan makes you look slimmer. But it's true that we've also actually got slimmer. I'm carrying less fat under my arms, and my calf muscles are visible now. Cycling hundreds of miles, of course we were going to lose weight.

"Miss Laplanche, you're a role model for all the young girls who follow the *Teen Dieting* blog. They're teenagers like you, and, like you, they don't like what they see in the mirror and would like to lose weight. They'd love to hear your story and find out how they, too, could get rid of those pesky extra pounds... May I ask you a few questions?"

"Absolutely not."

And get lost, I add silently, biting into a chocolate ice cream.

The mayor offers to put us up for free in a hotel room. We say we can't possibly accept, it's really kind of them, but no. But they won't let us say no; and the next thing you know, lo and behold, we're in a *hotel*!

"Look, Mireille! There's even conditioner!"

The shower is warm, the walls devoid of soapy smears. Happiness is your skin freed from ten centuries of dust, sweat and sun cream. I get rid of my underarm hair with a disposable razor. The shampoo smells of laurel, the conditioner of rosemary. I rinse my hair until it squeaks under my fingers.

When I emerge from the bathroom, Astrid is spread out on the huge bed, the TV on, sipping a cup of tea.

"What's on? Anything good?"

"No, just one of those home-video shows."

"Great, just what we need."

We fall asleep in front of the TV. A dog bites a lady's bum while she's cleaning the pavement outside her house; she drops her broom, which hits a passer-by on the head. Hilarious!

I wake up later, dragged from sleep by the jingle of the midnight news. Oh, Astrid, Hakima, the Sun—your ears must be burning in your dreams: they're talking about us, right from the start. The Three Little Piglettes are in Briare; they're going to Montargis tomorrow. My pumpkin face, giving an interview. Snippets from supportive Twitter and Facebook followers. A screenshot from the Nevers campsite's CCTV, where Malo can be seen jumping over a tent. Our sausages cooking, people licking their fingers. That mustard sauce is delicious! A sociologist explains why we fascinate everyone so much. Élise Michon, mayor of Paris: "We will be delighted to welcome these three young women to Paris." But what are they going to Paris for? It's a mystery...

"THREE LITTLE PIGLETTES" GEARING UP FOR A STORMY RIDE

Mireille Laplanche, Hakima Idriss and Astrid Blomvall set off this morning from Briare, in the Loiret department, for what might be a very long day. They are expected at midday in Montargis for a lunchtime sausage sale, and should reach the forest of Fontainebleau this evening.

The weather forecast is bleak, with storms predicted south of the Île-de-France region, but our three heroines aren't feeling low. "Come thunder, lightning or rain, we'll get to the outskirts of Paris on 13th July in the evening, and to the heart of the capital at midday on the 14th," Mireille Laplanche assured us. The young girls have reiterated, in response to widespread speculation, that they have no intention of disturbing the military parade for the national holiday. Meanwhile, in Nevers, Superintendent Tristan, in charge of the investigation into the Three Little Piglettes' bike sabotage, has announced that the police have identified a suspect, caught on CCTV at the campsite.

H.L.

("Hello?"

"Hello, Mireille? Hi, it's... it's Denis, Malo's dad."

"Oh. Hi."

"Mireille... a few days ago, Malo left Bourg-en-Bresse by car, with his cousin Félix driving. They told us they were going windsurfing in the South, but... we think we recognized Malo on the videos from the Nevers campsite."

"Oh, did you? Funny that."

"Mireille, listen, I... I'm so sorry about what happened. You... you know Malo lost his mum when he was young. You remember? He's a bit... unstable. He doesn't get on with my new girlfriend, and... you see, we're a bit worried, and we were hoping that maybe, if the police ask you questions about him, you might... I don't know. Go easy on him?... Mireille?... Are you still here?"

"Yeah, I'm still here. Do you remember the time when my mother went to see you after the first Pig Pageant?"

"Yes, of course. We did what we could, we told Malo—"

"And when she went back to see you again, after the second Pig Pageant?"

"Mireille, we really are so sorry—"

"And when your wife... passed away, when we were in Year 3, do you remember how I dropped by to see Malo every day, with a different cake each time?"

"Yes, Mireille. I remember. I... to be honest, I can't see any reason why you'd want to give him a break... But...")

223

21

And what would *you* do, dear reader, in my place?

What would you do if your ex-best friend, in whose company you used to make big playdough willies at nursery, if that former friend, after turning his back on you, after having you voted the school's number-one Pig for two years running, and then number-three Pig the next year; after trying to sabotage the cycle trip you organized in the hope of getting back some of your dignity; what would you do if that ex-best friend, pale as sliced aubergine and shaking like a bunny rabbit, chased by the police, suddenly appeared around a street corner right in front of you as you were going to the loo, during your lunch break?

What would you do if you saw him there, holding a lame little knife, his face streaked by two greasy, grey tear tracks running from the top of his cheeks to his chin?

Montargis. 1.15 p.m. Public toilets on a deserted street.

On the square at the end of the street, the other two piglettes and the Sun are chatting with our fans and filling them up with sausages. I said "Youokkader?" and

he said "Yeah I'm fine". "And Hakima, is Hakima OK?"
Hakima's belly is aching less now—Astrid's been feeding
her ibuprofen like sweets. Astrid said: "Wow, Mireille,
what's with the caring attitude all of a sudden? You
never used to care whether we were OK or not." I said:
"Let's be very clear, Astrid, I'm only asking because I
wouldn't want us to get delayed." Then I said I had to
go to the loo.

So here I am, on that deserted street, a strong smell of
piss rising from blackish stains on the asphalt; cardboard
boxes piled up by a STOP sign; boarded-up windows;
Malo, glaring at me.

"Malo. What are you doing here?"

"I warned you," he hiccups. "I warned you I'd gut you
if you made fun of me."

He's sobbing jerkily, like someone's giving him spo-
radic electric shocks; his shoulders are shaking. A pearl
of snot is dangling out of his nose.

"I can't see how I'm making fun of you."

I spread out my arms as if to say "Calm down, I'm
not armed." Survival instinct: zero per cent. If he tries
to stab me, as he seems to be intending to, I won't be
able to protect myself. I might end up losing my liver or
something. Unless my fat layer is thick enough to protect
me. His penknife is small, after all.

"You're *[huge hiccup]* making fun of me, because..."

Now he's crying for real, wiping his nose and eyes
with his sleeve; he sniffles, the pearl of snot rushes back
in, and then comes out again.

He says very quickly, between two sobs, "You and the other two fucking pigs, you want to humiliate me *[hiccup]*, I know that's what you want, your bloody stupid mystery *[hiccup]*, you're going to get to Paris and say things about me, slag me off, say horrible things about me, slag me off and..."

Broken record.

Me, in a slightly shaky voice, "Malo, seriously, it's got nothing to do with you. We wouldn't even be thinking about you if you hadn't slashed our tyres."

He walks towards me, bursts into tears again. He's so much younger than sixteen, when he's crying, he's barely twelve or thirteen—the voice he had before it broke comes back, the voice of the little boy who used to come over to eat Philippe Dumont's home-made crêpes.

"The police... They're... they're looking for me..."

"Yeah, I know, but you kind of brought it on yourself, didn't you? Why did you come all the way up here just to bother us like that? If you'd stayed in Bourg, you wouldn't be in trouble."

"Everyone *[hiccup]* is laughing *[long, triple hiccup]* at me, cos you... *[end of the sobbing fit]*... took that word 'pig' back and started using it..."

"Sorry, we didn't realize you'd copyrighted it."

He stumbles towards me; I step back, and suddenly, he... he tries, in a pathetic kind of way, to *gut me*. It's a bit like being in a nightmare, the same blue blur—I have a lot of nightmares like that, where someone comes to try to kill me. The same thing always happens: the sudden

226

feeling of slipping out of my body, of being a pure spirit, entirely terrified, desperately trying to protect the fat fleshy envelope I've been given by genetics and sugar tarts.

"Jesus! Malo, *stop it*!"

Thankfully, I don't have much trouble keeping him at bay. He's not at all as keen on gutting me as he claimed in his little speech; he just scrapes my arm a little bit, and then he tries to aim for my shoulder, but I push him away.

Sobbing, staggering like a new-born foal on his long, crane-like legs, Malo steps back, squeezing his knife in his fist.

"Malo, where's your cousin Félix?"

"Félix's gone... He got scared... He left... me... alone..."

"Right, listen—just go to the police, OK? It's the best thing you could do. Whatever happens, you're too young to go to prison."

"I'm scared..."

"Come on, I'll testify in your favour. If you want, I'll even say it wasn't your fault, that I'd pushed you over the edge. We could just say... I know: we could say, for instance, that I stole something really precious from you when we were in Year 7, and that's why you hate me so much. So you see, that way, it's also my fault. We'll tell the police that, and they'll be more understanding."

He fixes me, his face frothy with snot and tears, his features deformed. He's really ugly, actually. He sits down on the ground, legs crossed.

"No-o, Mireille, stop it, for God's sake, stop it..."

"Stop what?"

He drops his knife, which I quickly pick up—I'm not crazy—then I crouch down next to him. He's sobbing very hard, his head between his hands, and starts telling me off (I'm summarizing all this for you) for being much too nice to him even though he's been a bastard for all these years, and for not punching him in the face right now to punish him (no thanks, I like to keep my knuckles intact).

Struck by divine inspiration and a very strong need to pee, I tell him: "Listen, Malo, I'm not a psychologist, but I feel like you're displacing onto me your own feelings of guilt for having become a little macho dickhead, who chose to signal his entry into adolescence by publicly humiliating his best friend from childhood, and who's now been sucked into a downward spiral where he has to keep up the act of being a tough guy even though the girls he tried to destroy don't give a toss about him, and instead of cowering in fear are in fact ignoring him, cycling across half of France and becoming popular without his permission. Am I right?"

He nods, still sitting, his head between his hands, his polo shirt wet with various lachrymal liquids, and keeps repeating something along the lines of, "I hate you, you fat whore, you ugly bitch."

"I know."

"No! You shouldn't be saying that, you should be saying, 'How can you do this to me when I've supported you through [hiccups] hard times?'"

"Why should I say that?"

228

"Because it would only be *[hiccup]* FAIR, damn it! Why aren't you telling me that?"

"Well, because, Malo, I... I don't know. I dealt with all that a long time ago, I guess. I don't care now that we used to be close. I don't care that I spent hours with you when your mum died. I don't even care any more that I lent you my parachuting Action Man and you lost it like a moron by throwing it off a cliff in Brittany."

"But you don't think *[hiccup]* that it's unfair, what I did?"

"Sure. But I won't punish you for it. You'd be too happy."

I leave him there, and go for a pee. When I come out again, he's gone. Everyone's been looking for me—where's Mireille, have you seen Mireille? Ah, here she is, at last! Mireille, where were you? Are you OK? Smiles. *Mireille, can we ask you a few questions, it's for the eight o'clock news...*

That afternoon, I learn via an excited phone call from Hélène Lesnout that Malo has given himself in to the police.

Looks like the weather forecast wasn't entirely wrong.

"Do they think it's funny to film us like that?!" Astrid yells.

Apparently, the journalists do indeed think it's funny. We're surrounded by three cars and a bunch of smelly, noisy motorbikes, all with cameras pointing straight at us, and only pride is keeping us going forward. The rain is horizontal, scratching our cheeks—the wind pushes us back, when it doesn't suddenly blow us to the sides of the road. But that's nothing, really, when you consider the spectacular thunder and lightning all around us, adding a touch of apocalyptic excitement to the journey.

"Are we nearly there yet, Mireille?"

"Nope, Hakima, not yet..."

On the GPS, our "current location" remains stubbornly static, because we're going three times slower than usual. The little black-and-white chequered flag marking today's destination, the forest of Fontainebleau, isn't even in sight on the screen yet. My arms and legs have become bags of needles.

I know, I feel, I sense Astrid and Hakima's pain, too. I know them so well, now—I know so well their rhythms, their breathing patterns, the tempo of their tiredness—that I can feel, as if it were mine, by the minutest shifts in pedalling strength, that cramp in Hakima's left calf, that stiffness in Astrid's ankle. Their ragged breathing and exhausted coughing fits are mine, too.

How can the Sun keep propelling himself forward in that deluge, only using the strength of his arms? His body must be on fire from all the rain and sweat.

"We're going to get struck by lightning!" Hakima cries. She's right.

We get struck by lightning.

That'll be a good video for BFM TV's website: lightning strikes the Three Little Piglettes' trailer! I bet the solar charger's dead, now. And the fridge, uh-oh, I hope the fridge's still working... We're OK, yes, thank you. We've got rubber tyres, so we were protected. Safe and sound. We're not the kind to get struck down like that, no sir. Nothing can stop us.

It's almost midnight when we reach Fontainebleau, much too late to sell sausages, much too late to answer journalists' questions. I fall off my bike, drenched, drag myself to the barely unfolded tent, and then...

...I can't sleep.

I can't sleep, because my legs are still rehearsing today's endless pedalling; motionless, I pedal, pedal, pedal; I fall asleep for two minutes and dream that I'm pedalling; I awake with a start, turn to Astrid...

"Are you dreaming you're pedalling too?"

"God, tell me about it, I just can't stop pedalling in my head."

BIG BAD WEATHER HUFFS AND PUFFS
BUT THREE PIGLETTES PEDAL ON

After a stormy afternoon that Mireille Laplanche called "nightmarish", and during which the convoy was struck by lightning, the three teens and their companion Kader Idriss will be leaving the forest of Fontainebleau this morning to reach Choisy-le-Roi by the evening, where they will be spending the night. The young cyclists and their now-famous trailer will follow the winding course of the River Seine and have not specified where they will be stopping for lunch. The mayor of Choisy-le-Roi has already announced that Laplanche, Blomvall and the two Idrisses will be invited to stay at a hotel in the town. Speculations continue to abound as to the purpose of the three young girls' journey—that purpose should be revealed tomorrow, 14th July, when they get to the centre of Paris.

H.L.

Le Point @lepoint
Breaking: #3littlepiglettes Nevers sabotage: bike-slasher revealed to be organizer of Pig Pageant http://...

L'Express @lexpress
"I thought they wanted to make fun of me": Malo, 16, surrenders to police after #3littlepiglettes bike sabotage http://...

Le Figaro @lefigaro
#3littlepiglettes are the symptom of a deep crisis in the French school system: analysis by educational specialist Nathalie Polonais http://...

Metro @metro
Inspired by brave #3littlepiglettes, other "ugly" teenagers speak up about school bullying http://...

Grazia @grazia
Our summer #beauty tips: how not to be elected #pig of the school! http://...

22

This morning Astrid has a cold.

"It bust be because of the storb yesterday," she moans, wearing the saddest face in the world. "I'b pretty sure it's todsillitis."

"Tonsillitis! Why not leprosy, while you're at it? It's just a cold."

Her ears and throat are inflamed—the back of her mouth, when she goes *aaaah*, is bright red; the little dangly thing at the top of her throat looks like a big strawberry. I try my best to be very compassionate and sympathetic, but I can't help it: I *hate* people sniffling.

"Astrid, I beg you, blow your nose instead of sniffling."

"I'b like to see you try to blow your dose while cyclig!"

"Well, try to do it with one hand! Listen, it's pure horror—every time you sniffle, I have this vision of a slug of snot climbing up your nostrils and diving into your stomach."

"It's dot by fault if your ibagidation is hyperactib!"

The Sun intervenes. "We're not late, Mireille. We could take a break for a whole day and we'd still be on time tomorrow for the party."

"Absolutely *niet*. We're already going at tortoise speed because of Astrid's faulty immune system. I'd like to remind you all that *hotel beds* are awaiting our beautiful bodies in Choisy! And we must keep going—if we slow down now, they'll all say we're wimps and softies."

"Whatever we do, Astrid can't sell sausages in that state," Hakima says. "She'll give everyone tonsillitis."

"It's not tonsillitis, it's a cold. Come on, focus."

The banks of the Seine aren't as wild as those of the Loire. Fields have been replaced by promenades, herons by pigeons, cyclists by pram-pushing parents. We slip from suburban town to suburban town, and to me it all feels very new, that grey river fringed with tower blocks, small shops, teens sitting on the ground, smoking and catcalling. I'm used to villages and provincial towns, not to stretches of cement with the occasional friendly tree.

It doesn't smell of anything any more. I know some people say Paris stinks of smoke or piss or pollution, but what strikes me as we get closer to the capital isn't the smell, it's the absence of smell. I close my eyes while cycling and sniff the air, but I can no longer catch the dusty whiffs of cereal fields, the tart tang of stagnant water or the fresh, fatherly scent of thick-rooted oaks. Above all, the odours aren't blended together any more—smells here come one after the other: dog turd; pizzeria; dustbin; women's perfume; exhaust pipe. They don't mingle, they keep to themselves.

Hakima: "Why do so many people live here when there's so much space in the forest of Fontainebleau? And it's much prettier."

"Yeah, but it's further away..."

"Further away from what?"

(Snapshot from this morning, as we left the forest of Fontainebleau. We had to keep still for ten minutes, waiting for a great big stag to get up from the middle of the road, where he'd sat down.

"It's like id *Safari Park IV*," Astrid sniffled. "You always have to stop to let the adibals go through, they're always getting id your way."

I'd never seen a stag so close up. He was as thick across the chest as a horse, with the same swollen belly, but such long, thin legs, and velvety skin, stretched like hosiery over each muscle, each bone. He stood up clumsily, his head swinging, and went away calmly to nibble at lichens on a tree.)

"Further away from Paris," the Sun said, answering Hakima.

"But what's in Paris that people like so much?"

"You'll see... Paris is amazing."

"How do you know, Mireille? I thought you'd only been there when you were a baby."

"Yeah, but I've visited almost all of it on Google Street View."

Damn: the GPS won't switch on. Since that lightning

bolt speared our solar panel, I haven't been able to charge our precious travelling companion.

"Darling piglettes, we've lost our compass. We'll have to keep following the river and hope for the best."

The courageous convoy isn't in the happiest of moods today. The Sun is seriously starting to tire. This morning, I said, "Youokkader?" and he said, "Hmm, apart from some soreness in my arms and shoulders," and, knowing him, it must be much worse than he says. Of course, he probably didn't manage to take care of his stumps in Fontainebleau... I would gladly have helped him put out the daily fire, but he didn't ask, and I can't just force my budding firefighter skills on him. Meanwhile, the abominable Astrid is still sniffling and sneezing, and Hakima, instead of pedalling hard, is wasting a lot of energy saying "Poor Astrid, it must be awful, Mireille, honestly, we should stop, poor Astrid." I'm the only one still waving to the passers-by who recognize us.

Bridge after bridge, town after town, under a tin sky, along the tortuous river—let's just say it's not the best day of the journey.

When we finally decide to stop, we don't get a lot of customers; no one's brought us any dishes of cheese or chocolate. Hélène Lesnout had warned us: "You can't expect journalists to pay much attention to you today. They're all preparing 14th July features for tomorrow's news. All the underpaid interns who'd been following you hoping for a quirky story have been sent to military bases or aircraft carriers, or are interviewing the organizers of the Eiffel Tower firework display."

There are, though, a couple of motorbikes behind us when we leave again.

"Hi, Mireille, it's Mum. I've just read the news. You were *struck by lightning* yesterday?!"

"Oh yeah, I forgot to tell you that in my text this morning."

"But you're all OK?"

"Yes, we're mutants now. Our IQs have shot up by 100 points, and we can teleport from one end of the galaxy to the other."

"*[Sigh]* Mireille, the police came by this morning. They took a statement from us about Malo. And they... they said you'd talked to them?"

"Hmm, yeah, I talked to some cops this morning on the phone."

"They said you'd told them that a few years ago you stole a present from Malo that his mum had given him before her death, a photo album or something, and that you'd—that you'd burnt it."

"Oh yes. Shameful deed. Nasty piece of work, that Mireille."

"Mireille, you *lied* to the police?"

"They had to believe that Malo had good reasons to resent me, you see. Or else they'd be really harsh on him."

"You're much too nice to that little bastard."

"Yes. I've understood that it's in my best interests."

It's high time we got to Choisy-le-Roi: each strike of the pedal is a chore, each turn a torture. No one's saying anything any more. Hakima, I can tell, is increasingly tense, as if the Seine was a river of dribble carrying her straight to the belly of a monster. The Sun's behind us now, far behind—we stop almost every ten minutes to wait for him.

"You OK, Kader?"

"Hmm."

"Right! Let's stop."

"Are you kiddig be?" Astrid cries. "Whed it's one of us girls who've got big problebs, we doad stop, but if Kader's in paid, thed all of a sudded..."

"Who *has* got big problems."

She grumbles, but I can tell she's delighted to take a break. She and Hakima rush off to find a bakery.

Meanwhile, I sit down near the Sun, just in case he asks me again to help him. His mobile phone tinkles—email or text. He enters his pin—it's a Snapchat. I watch, from the corner of my eye, the three-second video. It's Jamal's girlfriend Anissa, filming herself in her bathroom mirror. Naked.

He switches off his screen and puts the phone down next to him. A ball of burning charcoal in my throat, I stammer, "If you like, I can leave you alone, I mean, if you've got things to look at."

He laughs. "No, thanks, I'm OK. I haven't got anything to look at."

"Are you, like... going out with Anissa, or what?"

"No, I'm not. She keeps sending me things. I don't reply. Jamal's been my best mate since childhood, you know, I'm not gonna steal his girlfriend."

"Are you going out with anyone?"

"Mireille, seriously... Have you taken a good look at me lately?"

"Yeah. Precisely."

He smiles and *tsks*, sadly. I carry on, full of energy. "But you could, right? I mean... Well, firstly, that's not the only thing that matters. But even if it was, you could, right?"

"You're so nosy! Yeah, sure, I *could*, since you're so interested."

Me, emitting a dramatic sort of cackle: "Ha! Interested! No, not *at all*!"

He bursts out laughing, of course, and I'm getting ready to throw myself into the Seine, but he starts again. "You know, I just don't meet very many people. I don't go out much. I downloaded Tinder—I tried but I got bored. At some point it showed me my French teacher from high school; it was so bloody depressing."

"Go out then. Go clubbing."

He shrugs. "Nothing's easily accessible, it's a bit shitty when you're in a wheelchair."

"Are you joking? You've just done hundreds of miles on the road, you went through gardens, campsites! You get by, I mean. You were *[big effort not to sound pissed off]* dancing, the other night, with that blonde girl. You could totally go clubbing and dance."

240

"Yeah, some day," he murmurs. "Someday I'll go dancing. When the results of the investigation have been published, I'll go dancing. When they confirm to me that I'm the victim in that story, yeah, I'll go clubbing. I'll buy myself prostheses too and try walking on my own. Until then, I'm in prison. As soon as they tell me I'm not guilty, I'll find myself a girlfriend."

"Guilty of what?"

"Of my friends' deaths. Of joining the army even though my parents didn't want me to. It was that compulsory day of military service you have to do at sixteen, you know? Have you done it yet?"

"No. Not yet."

"They showed us videos, they said it'd be great, that we'd do lots of humanitarian work, no real *conflicts*, no real fighting—that's not what the army does these days, they said. I was top of my class at the time, did you know that? But I decided to leave it all behind and join the army. I wanted to be that happy guy in those videos, hugging a little Somali boy he'd just saved, or some shit like that. Anyway, I join, and the first few years, it's that kind of stuff—and then suddenly *boom*—we're actually at war. Not much that's humanitarian about my job any more. And the first time I'm sent to a conflict zone, I fuck everything up."

"It was Sassin's fault, not yours."

"That's what I told my parents. Sassin... Sure, he should have predicted we were going to fall into a trap. But at the same time, once they started shooting at us, it was my job to react well. I could have... I shouldn't have... I don't know. See, I keep replaying it all in my head, thinking I could have given different orders, found another solution. I could have reacted differently."

"You weren't expecting it."

"Yeah, but that's normal for a soldier. Following orders, any idiot can do that—but reacting to things you hadn't anticipated, that's what sets you apart from the rest."

We stay there, enjoying the warmth of each other's company. We talk about ordinary stuff now; he tells me he really appreciates "what we've done for Hakima". Why, what have we done? Taken her under our wing, become her friend. She also became *my* friend, you know, and it's kind of her too. You didn't have any friends before? Kader asks. No. Well, none that I'd like to cycle next to for a week.

"Boo! We're back!" shouts Astrid. She's carrying a bag of *pains au chocolat* and a pop-music magazine. "Is Kader ady better, Bireille? You've bassaged his shoulders?"

Indochine are on the front page of the magazine. Astrid reads the whole article out loud, so we get a sense of what a monumental band they are, you see, it says it right there: *monumental*!

(Well, *bodubedtal*.)

We set off again.

There must be an airport somewhere close by, judging by the ear-splitting noise from the planes above our heads. Since my faithful GPS is asleep, I decide it's probably Charles de Gaulle. The Sun disagrees: it's Orly.

Astrid: "Hodestly, what do we care what airport it is!"

Hakima: "That's true, we don't care, the only thing we care about is that it's murdering our ears!"

At last, around 8.30 p.m., when the river's already black and the trees have swallowed up all the birds: "Smile, everyone. We're in Choisy."

And it looks like at least some people are interested in us here.

"Come, come, you can sell your sausages in the town-hall gardens!"

The town hall is a beautiful building that looks a bit like the Playmobil Victorian house. On a stage on the lawn, by the fountains, the residents of Choisy have chosen to welcome us with a brass band.

"Oh, no," Hakima whinges, "Mireille's done her thing again where everyone wants to take us around the city and talk about the historical monuments..."

But no, the mayor of Choisy has planned a relaxing kind of evening. After selling our sausages, we listen to the band, we talk to people. Some teenagers from the town go up on the stage for a spoken-word poetry show, and I'm a bit depressed because I'd like to be able to write things like that: hard-core, clever, interesting things about my life, with serious political statements inside, but I can't, because my life in Bourg-en-Bresse is just Mum and Philippe Dumont and the cat Fluffles.

I tell that to one of the poets, a tall guy called Zimo who slammed about his life and how he strives to get a grip on existence, a sense of balance, standing on top of glass towers for hours scrubbing and rinsing window-panes, sweating in five o'clock trains and feeling the pain of those around him, thinking of the figures he's seen flash up on computer screens through the windows as he works, six fucking zeros and here's him slaving two hours for twenty euros.

"Yeah, see, Zimo, I couldn't say things like that because it'd be a huge scam, seeing as my life's really easy and cool and I don't have to do anything apart from stroke my cat Fluffles."

That makes him laugh. "Wait, how old are you, fifteen? Even if you had interesting things to say, you wouldn't say them well. You can't say good things at fifteen, you're not mature enough. I see kids your age, they want to slam, but all they talk about is sex even though they've never had any, or prison even though they've never even smoked a joint."

The Sun says, "You'll write funny things, Mireille. You'll write things that make people laugh. That's your calling."

"I'd like to, but I can't," I say sadly. "I want the Nobel Prize in Literature, and they don't give it to funny writers."

"What do you want the Nobel for?"

"So I can fail to thank my biological father in my acceptance speech."

"Oh, right," say the Sun and Zimo, who understand, and respect my ambition.

Suddenly, a woman in her forties comes up to us to introduce herself. "Hi, I'm Valérie, but you've probably heard of me under the name of Simone Suffragette—the feminist blogger?"

"What!?" Astrid exclaims. "*You're* Sibode Suffragette?"

"Yes! Why is that so surprising?"

"Well, you haved't got, er..."

"Haven't got what?"

"You haved't got short hair like a bad!"

"She means a man," I explain.

"Well observed," Valérie/Simone Suffragette smiles.

"Are you dot a lesbiad?"

"Well, I... You know, you don't need to be a lesbian to be a feminist. Nor do you need short hair to be a lesbian. Or a feminist."

"Yes, but it helps, doesd't it?" Astrid counters.

Simone Suffragette laughs. "Listen, girls, I've been really looking forward to meeting you. I've been following you ever since I first heard of you on social media. You might know that there are two big causes I defend with particular passion. First, I'm fighting for the right of teenage girls not to be judged and criticized for their appearance, especially by boys their age. Also, I'm trying to get young women to see sport not as ways of losing weight, but as a path to self-fulfilment. The idea is to lobby politicians to get them to set up concrete policies that incentivize physical education practices which..."

(Here we go: Astrid and Hakima, those two ninnies, have drifted off. I can see their vacuous, intensely non-feminist glances spreading their tendrils buffet-wards.)

245

"...so, anyway—the three of you and what you've done are at the heart of those two struggles. That's why I'm so interested in you."

"Are you a Femen?" Hakima asks. "You know, those ladies who flash their boobs because of feminism?"

"Er, no, I..." (Simone Suffragette seems slightly surprised.) "You *do* know what feminism is, right?"

"Ask Mireille," Hakima says. "She tends to know about that sort of thing."

"I do, dear Hakima," I confirm. "Feminism is the idea that you're not born a woman, you become one. And that it's shitty to become one in a world where guys are still organizing Pig Pageants."

"Yeah, well, all *I* dow," says Astrid pointedly, "is that febidists are *very* excessive. By bother, for exabple, she's dot a febidist, because she says that febidists would like a world without bed, a world just with clodes."

"Claudes?"

"*Clo-des!*"

"Oh, right, a world without men, just with clones..." Simone Suffragette ponders those words. I can sense she's already writing a blog post in her head about our schools' failure to teach kids about what feminism really is. And about how the kids who know about it don't go around trumpeting their knowledge. Of course, I follow her blog, and those of other important feminists, and read books and stuff... but it's not like I'm going to run around screaming that I'm a feminist. Calling myself a *pig* is one thing. Calling myself a feminist would mean instant death.

(Just in case, though, I ask her how to join her activist group.

"Really, you'd like to? It would be amazing to have you with us, Mireille."

"Shush! Don't talk so loud, everyone'll hear us."

"So what? It's not illegal."

"No, it's worse.")

Later on, when night has fallen entirely and mosquitoes are feasting on us:

"Excuse me, young ladies?"

A tall man, who looks like an umbrella, very well dressed, small titanium glasses balanced on his nose.

"Very nice sausages. Allow me to introduce myself: Jules du Sty, counsellor to the president of the Republic."

We shake his hand, which is bony and moist.

"The president has sent me here on a special mission. She would be very honoured if the three of you and Monsieur Idriss would give her the pleasure of your company tomorrow, for the annual celebrations of the national holiday in the gardens of the presidential palace."

"What's that?" Hakima mumbles.

I translate: "He's saying [Barack Obamette] wants to invite us to the garden party at the Élysée tomorrow."

"Yeah but... yeah but..." stammers Astrid. "I thought we were supposed to..."

"Here are four official invitations in your names," says Jules du Sty. "Unless you are otherwise engaged."

He hands me the four official invites.

"No," I murmur. "We haven't got anything else planned. Literally nothing else."

"The garden party is at midday. Will you be able to find something to wear? The president and her family will welcome you on the steps of the palace before taking you through to the garden. There will be a short speech. You will then be able to talk to the president for no more than a couple of minutes—there will be in excess of four thousand people, mostly from humanitarian associations and sports charities. A buffet lunch will be provided."

"Where can we park our trailer?"

He pulls a face, glancing at our shiny vehicle from the corner of his eye. "I don't know. In the street, I guess, as long as it doesn't bother anyone..."

"But, Mireille, we were supposed to gatecrash that party tomorrow!"

"Yeah, that was the idea."

"But if we're invited... we can't gatecrash it any more!"

"I guess not."

"What do we do, then?"

"We face the unexpected. We accept the invitation. And once we're in, we stick to the plan."

"What plan? I'm confused. Is it still the same plan?"

"Yes. Three Little Piglettes, three objectives: humiliate Klaus Von Strudel, rip the Legion of Honour off General Sassin's chest and, for Astrid, meet Indochine."

Astrid, pensively: "Retrospectively, it's a pretty rubbish plad."

The Sun nods. Hakima too. I don't.

Even though, yeah, I must admit, that plan sounds a little rubbish now, after all the time and effort we've put into this.

The Bresse Courier, 14th July 20XX

PIGLETTES TO PARTAKE IN PRESIDENTIAL PICNIC

The three teenagers are like piglettes in the proverbial clover today, after receiving invitations to the prestigious presidential garden party at the Élysée Palace. Astrid Blomvall, Hakima Idriss, Mireille Laplanche and Kader Idriss will be entering Paris today and cycling straight to the palace.

The young girls are still expected to give their promised explanation as to the reasons for their journey: Mireille Laplanche assures that it will all become clear this afternoon. Several celebrity hairstylists and fashion designers have already announced that they would like to offer their services to the teenagers for free, ahead of the garden party.

H.L.

Jean-Paul Gaultier @jpgaultier_official
Jean-Paul Gaultier would love to dress the #3littlepiglettes **for the garden party—ITV** @lepoint http://...

Super Model News @super_model_news
How to dress elegantly if you look like #3littlepiglettes—Clarissa's advice http://...

Simone Suffragette @simonesuffragette
Sad to see so many people wanting to turn #3littlepiglettes into princesses.

Élysée Palace @elyseepalace
Official honours list for today's Legion of Honour ceremony at #garden-party http://...

"We're out of sausages."

"*Out* out?"

"Yep. We've sold everything. And out of a GPS, too."

"How much money have we made?"

"A lot."

"Are we really going to the Élysée garden party? We could see the sights of Paris instead!"

"Or go back to Bourg."

"No. The garden party's always been our goal. We're going."

"We could at least buy ourselves some nice shoes."

"No, we're staying in trainers."

"Why?"

"In case we have to run."

PART III

Paris

23

It's 9 a.m. when we get into Paris, 9.30 when we reach the Latin Quarter and stop by the Sorbonne. Why are we stopping near the Sorbonne, Mireille? Oh, no particular reason. OK, it's where my mother...

But it's just an old white building, that's all. I've heard it's nice inside. But it's closed today, because of the national holiday.

So we go for a walk, along pavements, through sunlight scattered by the branches above.

"How about *that*, Mireille, did you see *that* on Google Street View?" Hakima asks incessantly.

"Possibly. You know, it all looks the same. The only difference is that, on Google Street View, cars don't honk at you every five minutes and people don't run straight into you. They're standing still and their faces are blurred."

"Like that guy!" says Hakima, pointing at a man smoking under a porch.

Astrid's quietly pushing the Sun's wheelchair. The Sun whispered to me this morning that he thinks he's pulled a muscle in his shoulder. He asked me to massage his shoulder. I massaged the Sun's shoulder. I massaged the Sun's shoulder (repeat as many times as necessary). I said, "Apart from that, youokkader? Did you manage to put on some cream?" And he smiled and said, "Yes, Mireille, thanks."

I don't know if the massage worked. We had to stop at a pharmacy to buy him a heat patch.

"It's funny," Hakima says, "people don't recognize us much here."

To be fair, people don't really look at us. They walk through the heat and calm of the public holiday, looking up or down, but not at each other. Families, on the large Boulevard Saint-Michel, wear matching Bensimon shoes: his, hers and children's.

"It's beautiful!" (Astrid's ecstatic.) "Don't you think, Mireille, don't you think it's beautiful? Look at those buildings, they're like boats! Oh, look, there! A Space Invader!"

Her tonsillitis was remarkably short-lived, and she now has all the energy of a patient who's just recovered from a long and life-threatening illness.

Leaning against the balconies of the boat-buildings, people are making phone calls, smoking or staring at the horizon. Along the boulevard, the only places open are two second-hand bookshops, where customers flick through comics and paperbacks. So many dogs. Near a cash machine a little Roma girl's begging. Cars go through red lights. A couple brush past us; she's pissed off at him, but he couldn't care less...

"Look, Mireille, look, it's gorgeous, what is it? It looks like Notre-Dame!"

"It is Notre-Dame."

"Did you go there on Google Street View?"

"Yes, Hakima."

"Look, Mireille, those stained-glass windows, they're amazing—look at the colours..."

I don't know why Astrid's so excited and so remarkably unstressed. I guess she's just going to see an Indochine concert, not reveal to the world that Klaus Von Strudel is her father, or that General Sassin is a murderer. Hakima and the Sun, like me, are silent. We've got nothing to do until midday, apart from wander through the streets.

"Let's go and watch the parade, then."

We quickly get bored of the parade. We don't understand a thing, and the soldiers' hypnotic marching is exhausting to watch. The Sun, of course, knows exactly what's going on, which battalion's which and even some of the people there, and from his embittered face I can tell he'd rather be still propelling himself through the storm between Montargis and Fontainebleau than here, having to watch his former colleagues doing what he'll never be able to do again.

"Look, Mireille, look at the horses, how well they've dressed them up..."

Some people do recognize us and come to take selfies. A TV crew, bumping into us, ask us what we make of the parade. We let Astrid reply, since her opinions are exactly what they want to hear: it's magical, monumental, especially under this bright sunshine... Oh! Planes! It's amazing, look, they're leaving blue, white and red trails in the sky!

The journalists smile.

It's almost time. Question: should we, or should we not, accept the offers of the hairdressers and stylists who want to *help* us? My piglette self screams *no*—we have to go *just as we are*, like in Cluny, wearing our long dresses, our hair undone: the whole package, triple chin, pimples and all. Simone Suffragette's right: it's shameful that so many people would like to turn us into princesses.

But, of course... Klaus will be there, Klaus, to whom I'm going to say, *I'm your daughter*. The kind of occasion that would warrant a slight makeover, perhaps. Of course, deep down, I'd love to be able to *go as I am*. How easy it would be if I could afford not to wear a shadow of eye shadow, not a dab of foundation, and if people were still to say: "She looks like a princess, just as she is; it's not her fault, it's effortless, she's naturally beautiful; so it's OK, it's a feminist kind of beauty."

That'd be convenient right now.

"Look, Mireille, it's crazy—they're so synchronized! It must be so hard to learn to do that."

The soldiers' boots slam past, perfectly in time, their legs criss-cross like threads on a loom: clack, clack, clack. The Sun will never again be one of those threads on the loom. He can only clap. But he doesn't—nose up, he's staring at the TV channels' helicopters.

258

"It's not that hard, sticking to a rhythm," I say. "We've been doing it all week."

"Yeah, but not to that degree of precision... Oh, who are *they*?"

"Kids from Polytechnique," the Sun mutters.

The students from the elite university are wearing navy-blue uniforms, a little bit like Gab and Blondie's. They're very proud, you can tell, but they're careful not to smile. We keep clapping. A lady next to us says to her friend that her niece Léopoldine, who's a student at Polytechnique, will be marching in the parade next year.

"Come on, let's get out of here," the Sun grumbles.

We get out of there. Most of the streets are blocked— behind railings the riot police, like big beetles, are watching out for potential attackers. And so we wander between the boat-buildings for a couple of hours; we run into little parks; we drink the freezing, slightly sweet water of dark-green public fountains. Even Astrid isn't talking any more, after complaining for a while that we're *so dull*, the three of us, looking so *gloomy* in Paris, where we should be *enjoying* ourselves.

"Are you not stressed at all?" Hakima asks. "You're going to meet Indochine!"

"Of course I'm stressed! But I'm also... how can I put it... I'm like the milk you put into a cappuccino, you know? Super-stressed, but also frothy frothy frothy and full of little bubbles. You see what I mean?"

Miss Cappuccino-Milk ends up being the first into the public toilet we've found to get changed for the garden party. Public toilets in Paris are nothing like the stand-up, shit-smeared bogs you get in provincial roadside rest areas. They self-clean with a kind of water canon as soon as you leave. Of course, we weren't aware of that; Astrid helpfully leaves my and Hakima's dresses inside her cubicle for us, and when we open the door again they're drenched and smell of bleach.

We wring them under the small hand-dryer for half an hour.

"Are you really sure you don't want to ring the guy who said he'd give us free dresses, Mireille?"

"I'm sure."

We get changed. We look just as silly as we did in Cluny, and even crinklier, but we're more tanned and, yes, I guess, a bit slimmer. Doubtless *Teen Dieting* will write a feature about that.

While the Sun's getting changed, helped by Hakima ("Kader, I can help too, if Hakima's not strong enough"; "No, don't worry, Mireille, it'll be fine"), we put on some make-up and brush our hair, sitting near the arches of a very chic hotel, whose porter watches us with a look of pure disgust on his face.

I guess it's not entirely undeserved. Astrid swore she'd do me some "light make-up", but I end up looking like a kid who's had her face painted at a funfair. As a clown. Hakima managed to convince herself she had to put her hair up into a bun, even though her hair is absolutely unbunnable.

Finally, the Sun comes out again, pushed by his sister, his two empty trouser legs dangling. We walk slowly to the Élysée Palace.

Frankly, I haven't got the slightest idea what we're doing here.

But we're here now.

And a line of well-dressed people and journalists stretches out in front of us. We're going to have to go in.

"Right. Well, let's go in."

24

On TV, you often see the entrance to the Élysée Palace, with its red carpet unrolled on the gravel of the courtyard, and motionless guards, like little lead soldiers, on either side of the steps. You often see Barack Obamette standing there, in her severe, well-cut dress suits, her blow-dried black hair flecked with grey, shaking hands with other presidents from all over the world before the palace swallows them up.

Today, at the top of the steps, Barack Obamette is in red, flanked by the four men in her life: to her right, Huey, Dewey and little Louie, wearing almost-identical black suits; to her left, Klaus Von Strudel—namely, my father—in a light-grey suit, like his hair, like his eyes. Like my eyes.

In front of us, in front of them, a line of guests. I feel like I'm in *Cinderella*, when all the princesses are queuing up to be introduced to the prince in his ballerina tights.

"Are you going to scream out your big revelation here and now?" Hakima whispers to me.

My heart's beating in my lower lip, under my tongue, inside my ears.

"I don't know, it'd probably be better to get in first..."

The line moves fast, because it's just a very quick handshake: hello, introduce yourself, shake hands, go through. Klaus and the three boys only bow to the guests (Louie, you can tell, doesn't give a damn, but then he's only eight years old.)

"He seems in good shape, wouldn't you say?" a plump lady in front of us in the queue tells her husband. "He's less skinny. The remission must be going well."

"Hmm—you know, that stuff can come back at any point," the husband replies. "Especially if you first have it when you're young."

"He wasn't *that* young. He was, what, fifty-five? That makes me think, actually—weren't *you* supposed to get your prostate checked soon?"

"Anne-Cécile, for goodness' sake, keep your voice down."

What are they talking about?

I have no idea, so I butt in: "What are you talking about?"

Anne-Cécile and her husband (who's glaring at her now) turn to me.

"The president's husband," Anne-Cécile whispers. "He's just coming out of chemo for prostate cancer."

The Sun takes over, noticing that I can't utter a single word. "That's strange, we haven't heard anything about it."

"That's why my dear wife shouldn't be broadcasting it at the top of her voice. For all we know, you might be the editors in chief of *Elle*."

"Do we look like we're on the editorial board of a fashion magazine?" Astrid snorts.

"Oh! Wow! That's too funny!" Anne-Cécile clocks. "You're the Three Little Piglettes they've been talking about on TV!"

"Was the cancer bad?" I ask weakly.

"Oh no, it was a lovely, friendly little cancer!" Anne-Cécile chuckles. "Course it was bad. He was in treatment for months. That's why he couldn't be there when the King and Queen of England came. Poor man, he must have been all bald and skeletal, throwing up all the time..."

"Anne-Cécile, for heaven's sake, shut up..."

It's their turn: they're climbing up the steps, shaking hands with Barack Obamette—disappearing into the palace...

It's our turn.

"It's our turn, Mireille," says Astrid softly.

Since I'm not moving, she takes my right hand, and Hakima takes the left. I feel like I'm one of those little paper dolls, attached for life to her friends once the chain unfolds. An Élysée guard pushes the Sun's wheelchair up the disabled ramp, to the right.

Here they are. Barack Obamette's white smile and unsmiling eyes. Klaus's equally weary expression; the glazed looks on the three boys' faces.

I'm going to have to climb those steps, now.

I reshuffle my features, quickly and clumsily, into a happy expression.

"Miss Mireille Laplanche, Miss Astrid Blomvall and Miss Hakima Idriss."

Barack Obamette's hand, warm from dozens of previously shaken hands.

"It's a pleasure to have you with us today."

How many times has she said this in the past thirty minutes?

Itsapleasuretohaveyouwithustoday.

"Monsieur Kader Idriss."

"Itsapleasuretohaveyouwithustoday."

Desperately, I turn to Klaus; Klaus bows; I bow—his stare is empty. Yet he knows who I am, surely—he got my letters, he must have been following our journey in the news...

Surely our resemblance is blindingly obvious to everyone!

...I become blind myself, my vision blurred. Fatigue from the trip, and all the anxiety of finding myself here, on the Élysée Palace steps. Astrid's and Hakima's hands have found mine again.

"Everything all right, Miss Laplanche?" asks (my half-brother) Huey.

Two ribbons of tears unroll from my eyes; I nod, and leave with the others. We're taken to a garden. I would like to say—to *scream*—that I must absolutely talk to the president and to her husband, but I remain as dumb as a fish and almost as wet. With each breath, I half-drown in tears.

"We'll see them again later," whispers Astrid, who's now holding me by the waist. "You'll tell them later."

"He didn't recognize me," I try to say—but it comes out as a croak.

So I sit down on the corner of a bench in the garden, and I wait for Hakima and Astrid to get me something to eat and to drink.

I eat: six mini black puddings; four prunes wrapped in Parma ham; fourteen grilled almonds; three caviar canapés; three blini with smoked salmon; six tapenade canapés; five mini toast slices with foie gras; a small glass of avocado cream with chilli powder; two melon and prosciutto skewers; and three mozzarella and cherry tomato skewers.

I drink: a glass of Coke, a glass of pineapple juice, a glass of sparkling water, a Bellini and a glass of white wine.

I'm still not feeling great.

"Have a cry, Mireille. You're allowed to cry," says the Sun.

"I'm not crying!" I sob.

"Oh, OK then."

Then he does something that should pulverize me into a million soap bubbles: he puts his right arm around my shoulders and, with his (blistery) left hand, carefully dries my cheeks with a paper napkin.

And wipes my nose.

266

Great. The Sun's wiping my nose. Nothing sexier than all the snot in my body, pumped up from the deepest abysses of my lungs, going straight into his paper napkin.

Me: "Must have caught Astrid's cold."

"Clearly."

"Have I got mascara smeared all over my face?"

"All over. But it's cute, you look like a raccoon now."

"Brill. I was just thinking, not enough people come to the Élysée garden party dressed up as forest animals."

"It's a pity," the Sun confirms.

"If you want, I could lend you my eyeliner; you could go off and draw yourself a zebra face, and then we could run around screaming."

"You've got very nice eyes," says the Sun, brushing my locks aside. "I'd never noticed, because your hair's always in front of them."

OK. OK, fine. He's just said I have very nice eyes. OK, fine. My whole existence from now on will only be a long disappointment.

"I'd better buy a hair clip then."

"It would be a good investment," the Sun agrees.

"But if my hair doesn't fall over my face any more, everyone'll see me blush all the time."

"Is that why you keep it that way?"

"Partly. And also because, well, I'm butt-ugly."

"Oh, give it a rest. Firstly, some butts are very beautiful, and secondly...

So deep are your two eyes, my dear,
That as I drank their water clear
I spotted in one curvy globe
A Mireille shiny Suns disrobe."

"A Mireille shiny Suns?"

"Myriad. 'A myriad shiny suns disrobe.' As in, lots of suns. Louis Aragon, 'Elsa's Eyes'... Come on, Mireille, play along, for goodness' sake! I'm reciting one of the most beautiful love poems ever written; you should have an expression of pure rapture on your face."

"But wait, I don't get it—so the suns have come to look at themselves getting naked in her eyes or something? Because they make good mirrors?"

"Yes, that's right. Then later on he says:

"The brightest rays are those that pierce
Through the thick cloudedness of tears;
The eye is only at its bluest
When sadness paints the pupil blackest."

"What's that about?"

"It's, like, your eyes are all the prettier when they're crying."

"Oh, sod that. I don't like the idea that you're only beautiful when you're sad."

"Yeah, you're right, it's a stupid idea, actually." He sits up. "But don't worry," he whispers, they're also beautiful when you're happy. Like my sister, and Astrid. Six rays of sun. Look what you've done, this past week... You've lit everything up, wherever you've been. You've warmed people's hearts. Who cares about who's beautiful and who's ugly?"

"Everyone does. At least a bit."

"Yeah. A bit. Well, your eyes aren't running so much any more. That cold didn't last long."

"It was a very small cold. But I'm tired. I might go back to the hotel, or to Bourg-en-Bresse, or to my mother's belly. Do raccoons hibernate?"

"Have an espresso," the Sun suggests.

A few steps away from us, a penguin man armed with an espresso machine offers guests a *myriad* colourful capsules, like an attentive painter in front of his easel. At random, I pick a gold one.

Down it.

The coffee sinks its fangs into my throat.

"Better?" the Sun asks.

"Better, yes."

I am indeed feeling better. My brain is merrily mixing itself a cocktail out of all the drinks I've had these past twenty minutes, and I'm feeling better.

"Where's Astrid?"

"Over there, having a ball."

It's undoubtedly the best day of Astrid's whole life. Standing in her long dress, her face tomato-red, she's chatting animatedly with an oldish, skinny gentleman with a Sonic the Hedgehog hairstyle.

"It's the lead singer of Indochine," the Sun explains.

"I'd guessed. Has she taken pictures with him?"

"Approximately fifty-eight. She also got him to sign her T-shirt."

"Poor guy..."

But the poor guy doesn't seem too annoyed that a hysterical sixteen-year-old fan has Sellotaped herself to him since the beginning of the garden party. He's actually talking to her, and his smiles seem genuine. He's introducing her to other people, maybe musicians from the band. And, strangely, she hasn't spontaneously combusted yet; she says hello and keeps talking, her face entirely red like a giant raspberry, her hair straw-yellow.

If her Swedish father suddenly reappeared, I don't think she'd give a damn.

"At least *someone's* having a good time."

"Hmm," the Sun hmms.

"How about you? Have you spotted..."

"Yeah."

I'm guessing he spotted him a long time ago. *He's* standing over there, in full dress uniform, with his wife, next to a bush. He's eating, drinking and chatting with other military people, and another man I recognize, a government minister perhaps. He's glittering with medals.

"What are you going to do?" I ask the Sun.

"What am I going to do... You ask some funny questions."

"Are you going to talk to him?"

"To say what?"

"I don't know. Aren't you going to... to rip off his medal, or..."

270

He rolls his eyes. "Rip off his medal! Bloody nonsense. Childish talk. That's the kind of thing you can say when you're in Bourg-en-Bresse, sulking in your living room, not in the Élysée gardens."

I'm about to reply, but I feel a sudden stabbing in my throat as I see Klaus arriving. He mingles with the crowd, greets the guests. He joins the bunch of people around Sassin. They laugh. They *laugh together*. Klaus jokingly pretends to pull off Sassin's Legion of Honour medal; Sassin puts an imaginary gun to Klaus's temple. They're having fun, they're having so much fun!

"Where's Hakima?" the Sun asks, transfixed.

We look around: no Hakima.

And suddenly she appears.

She walks over and *plants herself right in front of Sassin*.

"What is she *doing*?!" the Sun chokes.

We look on, fascinated. It's like a silent film: little Hakima introducing herself to Klaus, then to Sassin, then to Sassin's wife, then to the minister and to the other people in the group.

"What the hell is she doing?" the Sun repeats...

"Finishing her therapy," I whisper...

A few minutes later, Hakima turns and points our way. We see Klaus and Sassin spot us, nod, smile—then they make their excuses to the other people in their group, before striding in our direction.

"I'm going to throw up," I warn the Sun.

271

"Me first," he says.

But the promised throwing-up fit fails to occur. Instead, I grab the Sun's hand, and we merrily crush each other's knuckles while Hakima, Sassin and Klaus keep walking towards us, for roughly forty days and forty nights.

Sassin's first words: "My dear Kader! How happy I am to see you."

"General." Kader salutes him.

"Call me Auguste, please. Miss Laplanche," says Sassin to me, and bows briskly.

I nod, and focus my attention onto the general's shiny Legion of Honour medal, frozen to the core at the thought of meeting Klaus's eyes.

"My dear Kader," repeats Sassin. "I followed your journey in the media, you know. I'm very happy to see that you... How shall I put it? That you're back in the game."

I stare at the Sun, my heart balanced on the tip of my tongue. It's now or never! He has to say it. *You can keep your praise. You killed my friends and sliced off my legs. Where were you when. Why didn't you. You must have known. How did you fail to predict. It's murder under another name. Where were you, Sassin, where were you when.*

In the end, though, the Sun just nods. "I had some help from those three young women."

"May I conclude," asks Sassin hurriedly, "may I conclude that you are at last accepting my offer, and that of the president?"

272

The Sun lowers his head.

Klaus turns to Sassin and asks, "What offer?"

"Well, for a whole year we've been trying to convince this young man to accept the Legion of Honour. No one deserves it more than he does. I assume you will be talking to the president tod—"

"No," the Sun chokes, "no, that's not why I'm here. I'm just here to accompany my sister. I'm here to be with Hakima."

Hakima, like me, is very still, utter stupefaction locking her jaw into place.

"For heaven's sake, Kader!" the general cries. "It's time to move on and accept what happened. You were heroic that day, everyone told you so." He explains to Klaus: "As he was lying there, his legs riddled with bullets, he managed to send radio messages to all the other troops that were out that day, telling them they were heading straight into a trap. Without him, we would have lost dozens of men."

"We lost ten," says the Sun darkly.

"Yes," says Sassin. "And they all got the posthumous honours they deserved. *You* haven't, Kader. I understand you've needed a bit of time, but now..."

"I'm waiting for the results of the inquiry," the Sun croaks, very pale.

"The inquiry will show that you acted impeccably. Responsibility for those deaths lies elsewhere. I am to a very large degree guilty, and, as you know, not a day goes by when I don't think about it."

"It wasn't your fault, General," says Kader, raising a face drained of all blood, his eyes shiny. "You couldn't have known."

"But I should have anticipated it. Kader, as you know, I only want to see you accept the honours that you are owed. You've received my many letters. You know my position. That day, that tragic day, you did exactly what you should have done."

Noticing the Sun's stony face, he takes his arm. "Come. Let us talk about it together."

They go off. Hakima, astounded, sticks around for a few seconds. Then she realizes she's in the middle of a potential father-daughter duel, and says, "Oh, sorry, I'll just leave you to it," and scuttles away like a little mouse.

The president's husband, one hand in his pocket, the other curled around a glass of champagne, gives me a kind smile. "Miss Laplanche. Mireille, am I right?"

I nod.

"You look confused."

"No, I... I'm just surprised, because... because we all thought that the Sun, I mean Kader, had been the victim of... well, we didn't know at all that Barack Ob... that your wife had offered him the Legion of Honour. We thought the general was... well, a... well, I'm just surprised."

He nods and sips his champagne, looking around, probably for some excuse to stop talking to me.

"Laplanche," he ponders. "Any relation to the philosopher?"

274

My ears are ringing. "What philosopher?"

"Jean Laplanche. A great thinker, psychoanalyst, philosopher. You're not related to him, by any chance?"

"No."

"Pity."

My brain's shouting to my mouth, "Come on, open, say something, come on, what use are you if you don't speak?" and Klaus is looking around again, he'll leave if I don't hold him back. "Come on, damn it, think of something to say!"

"Apparently," I cry out in desperation, "apparently I do look like a philosopher..."

"Oh yes? Who?"

He's staring at me.

You, you idiot.

"Jean-Paul Sartre."

That tickles Klaus. A lot. "Jean-Paul Sartre! Why not Socrates, while we're at it? What cruel person told you such a thing?"

"Friends."

"You should make other friends, young lady. I have heard that you like to call yourselves, erm... 'piglettes', but as far as I'm concerned, you're perfectly graceful and charming, and—"

"You know my mother. I'm sorry to interrupt. You know my mother."

"Do I? It's quite possible. Who is your mother?"

"Patricia Laplanche."

A tiny sign. Something. His eyes widening, almost

imperceptibly. Starbursts of wrinkles around them, stretching.

A tic in his cheek.

He stays silent for a while, and then takes a sip of champagne.

"Patricia, of course," he whispers. "I hadn't made the connection. I—yes, I supervised her excellent thesis on the concept of time in Nicolas Grimaldi's philosophy. It was many years ago, I can't remember exactly—"

"Fifteen and a half years ago."

"That sounds about right, yes. Patricia. Of course."

He finishes his champagne.

"And, so, what is your... your mother up to these days? I don't think I ever bumped into her again after her doctoral defence. We... wrote to each other two or three times, and then we lost touch."

"She's a philosophy teacher in Bourg-en-Bresse."

"Teacher? At a university?"

"No, high school."

"Is she? Very good," he murmurs, sounding like he doesn't think it's very good. "She was very talented, very creative and rigorous. She had potential as a philosopher. Do you have any... any brothers and sisters?"

"Not yet, but she's expecting another kid. A boy."

"I see. Very good."

He scratches his earhole, which doubles up as a vase for a little bouquet of grey hairs.

"There's going to be quite a gap between the two of you. How old are you?"

"Fifteen and a half," I answer, imploringly.

"Ah. Very good."

No use. It's not computing. He's not a mathematician, he's a philosopher.

So he launches into his favourite topic. "How about you, young lady? Do you like philosophy?"

My espressoed brain espresses me to say yes, of course I like philosophy, it must run in the family, *with the two of you as parents*, but instead I reply, "Yes, I do. I've read all your books."

"You've what?" He raises an eyebrow, surprised. "What do you mean, you've read my books? All of them?"

"Yes. My mother buys them and I read them too."

"Crikey. And you understand what they're about?"

"Some of the references I don't understand, but I haven't read all of Kant and Hegel, you see."

He laughs and slips his hand through what's left of his hair. "Good Lord, you're an unusual teenager. I'd love my boys to read my books, but they'd rather read comics."

"I like comics too."

"Very good. Very good."

"I wrote to you," I breathe. "Several times. Three times. I wrote to you three times. Didn't you get my letters?"

"I don't believe so. Where did you send them?"

"To the Sorbonne first, several years ago. Then to the Élysée."

"I'm sorry, I don't recall ever seeing them. Here at the Élysée the mail gets read by secretaries anyway—we hardly see any. So many people write to us. What did those letters say?"

"They said..."

I wish my head could stop spinning.

"They said I like your books."

"Did they? That's very kind of you. I would have liked to receive those letters."

He swings his head back to drink up an imaginary last drop of champagne.

"And your... well—your, ahem, your father, then—what does he do?"

I stare at him. Has he *really* not made the connection? His grey, impassive gaze meets mine calmly. Did he *really* never receive my letters?

Noticing I'm taking a long time to reply, he goes, "I'm sorry, perhaps that's too personal a question."

"No, not at all. My father is... my father is a solicitor. He's called Philippe. He's a solicitor in Bourg-en-Bresse."

"A solicitor? Oh. I see. Very well. And does he also like philosophy?"

"No," I say, a ping-pong ball in my throat. "It's not his thing."

"There must be other things he's good at," Klaus suggests.

"Yeah, there are. He... he makes very good crêpes."

Klaus smiles. "That's an important thing, being able to make very good crêpes."

I smile too, a real smile. "It is. And he helps me do my homework, without getting annoyed, unlike my mother.

278

He takes me to see exhibitions and walks with me in the forest. He takes me wine-tasting. He's the one who taught me how to make lasagne. And since Mum's job isn't very flexible, he was always the one looking after me when I was sick in primary school. He loses at tennis on purpose even though he's better than me. He takes me to the cinema. He repainted my bedroom last year. We went to Ikea and he let me have the lamp with all the multicoloured balls. When I was six, he gave me a kitten, who's now a big fat cat called Fluffles. He took me to the swimming pool every Saturday for a year so I could learn to swim all the different strokes. He didn't tell me off the time I dropped my chocolate ice cream on the new seats of his BMW when I was nine."

Klaus nods. "Well, you're a lucky girl. Your father sounds like a good man."

"Yes, I am. Yes. He is."

He nods again, still looking pensive.

"All right, young lady, I should probably be rejoining my wife—"

"Wait..."

My hand's clutching his arm.

"Wait, please. Just a moment. There's something I'd like to tell you."

"Oh, sure, please do! Do tell, do tell."

His smile is frank, friendly. *He does not know.* He *really* hasn't clocked anything. I'm sure of it now; he doesn't know. He doesn't suspect a thing.

"I... I am..."

"Yes? No need to be shy."

"I... I've got the manuscript of a philosophy book my mother's written."

"Have you?"

"I know I'm not a philosopher like you, but she is. I've got it here. I've read it, honestly, it's really cool. Well, I mean, not cool, but I don't know the right philosophical terms to describe it. Can I leave it with you? Please, do read it."

"Of course I will. I'm sure it's excellent. Let me see— *Being and Bewilderment: Towards a Philosophy of the Unexpect...*"

He grins, and a moment later I think his eyes are blurry.

"I believe I know what's in there," he says fondly. "Yes, I remember... We used to talk about it a lot."

He flicks through the book, looks at the dedication. *To my daughter Mireille.*

Klaus stares at me.

"I was very—I mean, how can I put it?... I was very close to your mother."

"So I've heard."

He coughs into a handkerchief. His face, when it contracts, looks older, more tired.

"It's rare, you know, when... when you find a student who's really able—not just to agree with you, but also to challenge you intelligently, to..."

He peers at the first few pages.

"That's right," he says. "Everything changes, unpredictably, and we must always react to the unexpected. I remember."

He keeps nodding, keeps smiling, looking a little silly, lost in his memories.

"I'm looking forward to reading it. Very much."

He fixes me, and behind him I spot Barack Obamette walking, very professionally, towards a group of guests. Louie's sitting on the floor, looking extremely bored. Huey and Dewey have found two tall blondes to flirt with.

Klaus lays his wrinkly hand on my shoulder. "It's a funny thing, life. I wasn't... I wasn't expecting at all to see this part of my existence re-emerge, today, at this tiresome social gathering. But I guess Patricia was always where I expected her least. It's a pleasant thing, sometimes, to be surprised."

He nods at his wife, who's just beckoned him over. He throws me one last look.

"She's right, you know, your mother—nothing can be entirely planned for. And she may be right, too, about it making us who we are. Certainly, I... yes, certainly, I'm suddenly feeling a little bit... more human."

He pats my shoulder, perplexedly, clumsily.

And then he goes his way and I go mine.

HAPPILY EVER AFTER: THREE LITTLE PIGLETTES TURN FAIRY GODMOTHERS

Mireille Laplanche, Astrid Blomvall and Hakima Idriss have at last explained, as promised, why they embarked on their sausage-selling journey across France. "The aim," Laplanche stated, "was to collect money for charities that matter to us."

All the money they earned selling sausages will be donated to charity, split between a war veterans' charity, a charity campaigning against school bullying and another promoting women's sports. Their notorious sausage trailer will be sold on eBay for the same purpose; it is expected to fetch upwards of €1,000. Since the Three Little Piglettes' endorsement of these charities, they have all reported a rise in donations.

The explanation was the cause of some surprise—indeed perhaps some disappointment—among Internet users, who were, it seems, hoping for a more spectacular justification. Feminist blogger Simone Suffragette, however, who has been supporting the Three Little Piglettes since 8th July, praised their initiative, underlining that the expectation surrounding the three teenagers' revelation had "achieved something that is no mean feat in a society obsessed by individualism and show business—they celebrated the values of solidarity, generosity and hope."

Not a bad ending to the Three Little Piglettes' tale.

H.L.

On the evening of 14th July, we watched the fireworks from the Trocadéro esplanade, overlooking the Eiffel Tower. When the last, monumental plume of blue, white and red flames dissolved in the night air, leaving just a cloud of a sparkly snow, we joined in with the rest of the crowd, applauding and kissing our neighbours on the cheeks.

Then we went back to our hotel. Astrid couldn't stop stroking her signed Indochine T-shirt. Kader and Hakima talked to their parents on the phone—mostly about Kader's potential Legion of Honour.

I was just tired, so I slept.

I dreamt I was pedalling.

The next day, we took a train back to Bourg-en-Bresse. The whole time, we discussed destinations for the next bike trip. Maybe to Bordeaux. But not selling sausages this time.

When we were back, when it was time to say goodbye, Hakima cried (even though we were going to see each other again the next day). Astrid was welling up too. What a pair of saps! I gave them my biggest smile and kept my own emotions tucked away inside, which is their rightful place.

Then Kader hugged me, kissed my cheek and whispered a *thank you* that spiralled down the circumvolutions of my tiny, weirdly shaped ear, and I had to go home quickly because all those bells ringing inside my skull were beginning to make me feel a bit tipsy.

—

We'll be going back to Paris.

We'll be going back to Paris for Kader's Legion of Honour ceremony. He accepted the medal, mostly to please Sassin, his parents and the nation. But to me, what matters is that, afterwards, he might finally buy himself some prostheses, go clubbing, dance, kiss girls. Be happy.

We'll go back to Paris for the next Indochine concert at the Stade de France—Astrid wrangled us four invites, of course.

We'll go back to Paris for the launch of *Being and Bewilderment: Towards a Philosophy of the Unexpected*, by Patricia Laplanche. There's going to be an evening of readings and nerdy talks in some stuck-up bookshop in the Latin Quarter.

(And guess WHO will have to give Julius-Aurelian his baby bottle while the intellectual lady and her husband swirl around drinking champagne and signing books? That's right, Mireille "Free Babysitter" Laplanche. Life lesson: have children fifteen years apart—it'll save you a lot of cash on the second one.)

Epilogue

At the end of the summer, Hakima, Astrid and I climbed up the Rock of Solutré. Easy-peasy for our muscular calves! We fearlessly crunched pebbles under our feet; we didn't blink when weedy blocks of earth tumbled down as we walked past; we laughed at other walkers huffing and puffing like steam engines. We took in the warm, heavy air, charged with dust, that the land breathes out every August evening.

At the top, we sat down on a flat rock and unwrapped our picnic. The whole countryside around was liquid black and orange in the light of the setting sun. We ate cold chicken thighs and cherry tomatoes, Crottin de Chavignol and grapes, *fougasses* studded with puffed-up olives, pistachio fondants as smooth as lava stone, and we drank apple juice straight from the bottle.

Eating and chatting, we watched the world solidify, grey-blue, as night fell, and then we lay down on the hard ground to count the stars.

"It was right here," said Hakima. "It was right here that the horses would gather when the cavemen chased them, all that time ago. They had to jump, because they were under so much pressure."

"Just imagine the pile of bones there must have been down there!" Astrid sighed.

"There's still some," Hakima said. "There's lots of horse bones, down there. Fossilified."

"Fossilized," I said. "Look, Ursa Major!"

I traced Ursa Major with my finger. A nice big frying pan, in which you could toss, for instance, a handful of duck livers with some raspberry vinegar, and then pop them into a salad.

(No sausages, please. We'll never eat another sausage as long as we live.)

Hakima: "How about the other constellations?"

"No idea. I only know Ursa Major. The others aren't shaped like cooking utensils."

"You're so uncultured," Astrid grumbles. "You can tell you weren't brought up in the mountains. That's Orion, with its belt. And that's Pegasus."

"Pegasus?"

"Yeah, you know, the flying horse, with the wings."

"The flying horse?"

Hakima sits up, as if to stare at the constellation closer up.

"*That's* the most horrible thing in the story, when you think about it," she says. "The horses would run all the way up here, and the men were egging them on, and they must have thought, *Shit, why haven't we got any wings? Why can't we just fly away, instead of falling down?*"

"Because that's *My Little Pony*, not prehistory," I said.

Astrid yawned. "Maybe some of them did have wings. How would we know? It's a bit like mythology, prehistory! People couldn't write at the time—they didn't spend their days telling their friends about what was happening in their lives. They couldn't have sent a message around, going, 'Hey, guys, listen to this, there's a horse that flew away instead of falling down, what a jerk!' It wouldn't have been front-page news."

Hakima lay down again, a smile on her lips. "Great, then let's say that's what happened. Let's say some of them got to the top, with men chasing them behind, and they flew away instead of falling down. The hunters would've been so pissed off."

I yawned too, beginning to fall asleep. But tall clumsy daddy-long-legs were landing awkwardly on my face, like tiny Pegasuses made from wire and string.

"I can picture them in my head," Hakima murmured. "I can see the ones who'd reached the edge and had to jump..."

I closed my eyes so I could see them too.

"...and among all the falling ones," Hakima continued in a voice that was barely more than a whisper, "I can see those that were pedalling, pedalling, pedalling, beating the air with their big hooves—until they realized that they'd grown wings, and they could fly away..."

PUSHKIN PRESS

CLÉMENTINE BEAUVAIS (born 1989) is a French author living in the UK. She writes books in both French and English, for a variety of ages, and is a lecturer at the University of York. *Piglettes* won four prizes in France, including the biggest book prize for young adult fiction, the Prix Sorcières. Film and stage versions are also in production. Now Clémentine has translated her book into English!